A Christmas Bodyguard Romance

HIDDEN Shadows

NYSSA KATHRYN

HIDDEN SHADOWS
Copyright © 2023 Nyssa Kathryn Sitarenos

An NW Partners Book
Cover by Deranged Doctor Design
Developmentally and Copy Edited by Kelli Collins
Line Edited by Jessica Snyder
Proofread by Amanda Cuff and Jen Katemi
Cover Photography by Andrey Bahia at Wander Book Club

❀ Created with Vellum

She doesn't want a bodyguard. He doesn't want to attend a Christmas fair. It should make for a memorable holiday.

Finley Dunkley hates flying. And more than that, she hates flying in the window seat. When she asks the stranger beside her to switch, she doesn't expect a blunt dismissal of her request. She also doesn't expect to fall asleep on his shoulder. It's embarrassing, but at least she won't ever see the man again...or so she thinks.

Former Navy SEAL Nixon Reid is accustomed to being obeyed. In his line of work, the difference between following orders and not can mean the difference between life or death. So when his new client challenges him at every step, he has to work hard to remain calm. Walking away isn't an option, not when she has a stalker and Nixon's promised to protect her. To make matters worse, it's almost Christmas. The time of year that incites his worst mood...and his worst memories.

As the days tick by, Finley is more and more at risk, and the couple struggle over their differences. With time running out, they need to find a Christmas stalker before he finds them first, putting a permanent end to Finley and Nixon's fragile truce...and fiery attraction.

ACKNOWLEDGMENTS

Thank you to my beautiful book team who edit and proofread my work, making sure it's the best quality possible – Kelli, Jessica, Amanda and Jen, you guys are amazing. Thank you.

Thank you to my ARC team who read my words first and fill me with confidence to release my work into the world.

Thank you to my readers, you are the reason the next gets written.

And thank you to my husband and daughter. Will and Sophia, you are my joy. You are my heart. And you are the reason I can do what I love.

CHAPTER 1

Finley Dunkley stepped onto the plane, her fingers trembling slightly as she held out her ticket to the flight attendant. Whatever the woman said was like white noise, the beating of her heart all she heard.

Man, she hated flying. It wasn't at a phobia level, but it was close. And while she loved her job as an event marketer, traveling was the only downside.

She tried to smile at the woman before walking forward but was sure it came out all kinds of wrong. Her eyes were down as she stepped into the aisle, and she was so in her own head that she ran smack dab into someone's chest.

Crap.

"I'm so sorry," she gasped as she looked up into the man's blue eyes. He barely smiled, just dipped his head and stepped around her.

She didn't have to go far. 2F. Both a business-class seat…and a window seat.

She dropped into her allocated spot, and her fingers immediately started a nervous strum along the plush arm as she glanced down the aisle. Nerves trickled up her spine—that whoever was sitting beside her would choose not to switch seats…that she'd be stuck beside the window for the entire flight.

If she'd booked this flight herself, she never would have booked a window seat. Hell, she wouldn't have even selected business class. But Beth, the organizer of the Christmas fair she was working, had bought her the ticket.

Why sitting beside the window made flying worse, she wasn't sure. Yes, there was a blind you could pull down, but no, it didn't dull the fear in her belly.

It was fine. She'd be fine. One quick flight to Fallen Ridge, Ontario, then the plane would safely land. There'd be no big crash. No headline news. And with any luck, no turbulence.

She leaned down and unzipped her bag, then pulled out two small pills and some water. Xanax. Sometimes the only thing that kept her nerves steady. On longer flights, the medication even helped her get some sleep, but this was a short trip, so the likelihood of that happening was low.

Her fear of flying seemed to have come out of nowhere. She'd even Googled it once. But she didn't have a past traumatic experience. She had an added fear of enclosed spaces only when she sat in the window seat. Maybe it was a combination of everything—small space, up high, no control of the situation, and reading too much news.

Thank you, media.

"Champagne, Miss Dunkley?"

She looked up to see a young flight attendant. "No, thank you."

The woman's gaze shifted to the bag at her feet. "I'm sorry, your bag is a bit too large for below the seat. Could you please put it in the overhead compartment?"

"Oh. Sure. Sorry."

As the attendant moved away with the tray of glasses, Finley grabbed the bag and stood. Her arm shook when she lifted it above her head, but that wasn't due to nerves.

Damn her and her inability to pack light. It was a two-week trip. But to be fair, she was flying into Ontario in December. There'd be snow and a lot of it. Which meant big, space-taking warm clothes were required.

She pushed the bag in, but it only went halfway before hitting resistance. With a frown, she shoved it again. Why wasn't it moving? She readjusted her feet to give it a third shove.

"There's something behind it." The voice was deep, gravelly.

Turning, she found herself staring right at a big, toned chest, then looked up, way up, into a set of dark, almost black eyes.

The man was huge. So huge that he reminded her of her best friend's military brothers. This guy even had that same intense look in his eyes, like he'd seen the darkest crevices of the world.

Oh, and he was beautiful, in a ruggedly sexy kind of way.

Her breath caught when he leaned over her, reaching behind her bag and pushing something aside. A deeply masculine scent permeated the air. It was a combination of sandalwood and spices…intoxicating. She peeked up to see his biceps flexing as he shuffled the luggage.

Oh, sweet Jesus…

When he was done, he lowered his arms, and it took her too long to realize she was in his way.

"Sorry," she muttered quickly, sliding back into her seat. "Thank you for your help."

But the man didn't continue down the aisle. He put a second bag in the overhead compartment, then slid into the seat beside her.

Her jaw dropped. She was going to have to sit beside this god of a man for the next two hours? Not only that, but he'd be witness to her little flying phobia?

She cleared her throat. "I'm Finley, by the way."

"Nixon."

Even his name was sexy. And that deep rumble of a voice that slid over her skin caused all the fine hairs on her arms to stand on end.

She swallowed. A big, clunky swallow that didn't come close to wetting her dry throat. "I'm sorry to ask, but would you mind switching seats with me?"

He turned his black eyes on her, seeming to consider her question for a full second before saying, "I'd prefer not to."

Her lips parted further. Not the answer she'd been expecting. The man didn't owe her his seat or anything, but most people would at least have given a reason.

She wet her lips. "I'm sorry, but the thing is, I hate flying. It's not at the phobia level, more a hyperventilate-unless-I-breathe-through-it level, so… close. And because the blind has to be up on takeoff and landing, this seat kind of makes it ten times worse."

Something flickered in his eyes, some emotion that looked a bit like sympathy and had hope skipping in her chest. Then he spoke.

"I'm sorry to hear that. But I can't swap with you."

The hope died, like a small flame that had been doused in water. And again, there was no reason given. Not even a pretty little lie about wanting to be closer to the bathroom or only liking the aisle seat.

A voice in her head told her to leave it. He'd said no. It was his seat, and he was entitled to keep it. But the words fell out of her mouth before she could stop them.

She angled her body toward his. "It's just that at check-in, I asked to be swapped to a non-window seat and was told it was a full flight. She told me to ask the person next to me when we sat down—"

"Finley." Her breath stuttered at the sound of her name on his lips. "I really commiserate with that. But I can't swap. And we're about to take off, so I'd suggest you put on your seat belt."

Right on cue, the pilot's voice came over the speaker.

Her lips snapped shut, frustration at the man beside her competing with the fear of flying. It wasn't that she felt entitled to his seat. He'd booked it—of course he could sit there. But the fear in her chest was as irrational as the rest of her, and right now that fear was telling her that this guy was a jerk for not switching.

For a second, she was tempted to lean forward and ask the person in the aisle seat in front of her, or hell, behind her, but the flight attendant started going through safety instructions.

Finley's heart began to beat faster in her chest. Her fingers continued to tremble as she fastened her seat belt. She counted in her head, a calming technique she'd used multiple times before.

In, two, three, four, hold...out, two, three, four.

The plane jerked a little as it pushed back from the terminal, and she gripped the arms of the seat like they were the only thing keeping her rooted to the spot.

Takeoff and landing...her two most hated parts of the flight. It all sucked, but the start and the end sucked the most.

She closed her eyes, focusing on her counting and the sensation of filling her lungs with air. It was only when the armrest beneath her fingers twitched that her eyes flew open and her gaze shot down.

Not the armrest...a real arm.

Shit.

She tugged her hand off. "Sorry!"

He removed his arm. "You can have it."

She muttered a thanks, even though a part of her was still irrationally angry at the guy for not switching with her.

His eyes remained on her. "You know, the chances of this plane crashing are—"

"One in eleven million. I know." She closed her eyes again. "I've got more chance of dying in a car crash. Safer in the air than on the ground. I've heard them all before."

But unfortunately, none of it helped. It was probably too rational for her muddy, fear-induced mind.

She was still focusing on her breaths when she felt the whispers of heat at her side. It was subtle, the man wasn't even touching her, but somehow she just felt like he was moving closer. Whether it was intentional or not, she wasn't sure, but the sensation made a tiny bit of the tightness release in her chest.

When they were finally in the air, she blew out a long-stuttered breath but didn't open her eyes. The heat at her side also didn't disappear. A part of her wanted to lean into it. To breathe in his woodsy sandalwood scent. Because for some reason, the man calmed some of the anxiety inside her.

CHAPTER 2

 ixon Reid's muscles tightened as the woman nuzzled her cheek into his shoulder.

Who the hell slept on a two-hour flight?

Obviously, the same woman who'd glared at him for not giving up the aisle seat and then again for trying to relay facts about flight safety.

He leaned his head back against the padded cushion, trying to ignore the way the warmth of her skin seeped through the material of her shirt and into his shoulder. To not watch the slow rise and fall of her chest or listen to the soft hum of her breathing.

She was beautiful, with her long brown hair and big brown eyes. Even while she'd been sending him angry side glares, she was still gorgeous. And she had this sweet scent of lilacs and honey.

His fingers tightened around his phone as he tried to concentrate on the words on the screen. Notes for the job he was doing in Ontario. It was damn hard, not only because of the woman beside him but because of the fucking Christmas music playing from her headphones. The volume was up so loud that all he could hear were the lyrics to "Let It Snow."

Fuck, he hated Christmas. Everything about this time of year made his skin crawl and his lungs pull so fucking tight he thought he'd never get a full breath in again. He'd wanted to turn down this job. Hell, he *had* turned it down. Fly to Ontario, at Christmas, and spend time at a fair called Winter Wonderland?

Fuck no. Everything about it sounded like his very own version of hell.

But the man asking him to do the job wasn't just anyone. He was a friend. A guy Nixon had served with. So when he'd pushed it, Nixon had gritted his damn teeth and agreed.

And he was already regretting it.

He forced his attention back to the notes on the phone, committing every detail to memory. Even if he didn't want to be here, he'd damn well do a good job. He treated *every* job like a mission, the former Navy SEAL in him never letting a detail slip, no matter how small. It was often the small details that could make or break a mission.

He'd wanted to be a SEAL since he was a kid, and not because of the notoriety or to impress anyone. He'd wanted to do it because in order to take down the worst scum on earth, you had to be the best. So that's what he'd become…the best.

A soft feminine noise sounded from Finley. It was something between a hum and a moan, and it made the muscles in Nixon's forearm twitch.

He ground his jaw and was just reading over the notes for the hundredth damn time when the pilot's voice came over the speaker.

"This is your pilot speaking. We're about to go through some clear-air turbulence. I ask that people ensure their seat belts are on. Cabin crew, be seated."

The pilot had barely finished speaking when they hit the first bump. The plane shook, a couple of gasps sounding from guests around him.

Finley's breathing shifted from long, slow breaths to shorter ones. She nuzzled her face into his shoulder before reaching up and rubbing her eyes. When that hand slipped from her face to his biceps, she froze. Then, slowly, she looked up until her eyes collided with his.

Her jaw dropped, a pretty pink shading her cheeks. She seemed like she was about to say something, but before any words could come out, the plane shook again. She gasped, the fingers that were still around his biceps tightening and the pink stain in her cheeks fleeing as her skin turned pale.

"We're going through some clear-air turbulence," he said, voice too damn gruff.

"Turbulence?" Her voice was high-pitched, and she said the word like it was a death sentence.

"It'll be fine."

"Fine." She nodded, but the action was too vigorous. "Yeah. We'll be fine."

She peeled her fingers from his biceps and grabbed the arm of the chair. Just like on takeoff, her knuckles whitened and her back was unnaturally straight.

She swallowed. "I mean, I would believe you, but there's no way you could *actually* know that. I'm sure in every plane that's ever crashed there's been the person onboard who told people it would be fine, and then it wasn't." She leaned against the cushioned headrest. "If this plane crashes, then it's the worst timing. I haven't traveled enough. I haven't conquered this fear of flying. I always wanted to teach but never did that. I haven't adopted a rescue pet or fallen in love."

"You'll be able to do all of that."

"Maybe…hopefully."

The plane shook again, but this time more violently. When the remaining color in her face leached away, Nixon cursed quietly before reaching out and slipping his hand over hers. "Hey. Look at me."

It took her three heartbeats before her big brown eyes connected with his.

"I've got you. You're safe."

Her brows flickered. For a moment, he thought she was going to tell him again that he couldn't promise that. But then she turned her hand over in his and interlaced their fingers.

His heart thudded, and he had no fucking idea why. Because she looked at him, *touched* him, like she actually trusted him to keep her safe? Because this stranger was leaning on him for comfort and he liked it?

She didn't take her gaze from his eyes, and he didn't shift his own from hers. She watched him like he was her lifeline. The only thing keeping her calm and grounded.

The plane continued to rock and shake around them, more gasps and murmurs sounding from other passengers, but their connection never broke.

It was three minutes of turbulence before the plane finally steadied.

A long breath released from her. "Is it over?"

Before he could answer, the pilot's voice came on again, telling them they were through the worst of it.

"It's over, honey." The endearment slipped from his lips before he could stop it.

"Thank you," she whispered, before leaning her head back and closing her eyes.

She untangled her fingers, and the second their touch ended, he was left wondering why the hell his hand twitched to reach back over and take hers again.

CHAPTER 3

Finley watched the snow hit the ground from the back seat of the hotel transfer car. Her cheeks were still flaming hot from waking up with her head against Nixon's shoulder and then from her near panic attack.

God, she'd been a mess. She scrunched her eyes closed, as if that could somehow erase the memories.

Figured that she'd be seated beside the hottest man on the plane, only to thoroughly embarrass herself. She'd barely been able to look at him after that. Even when they parted, all she'd managed was a muttered goodbye before hightailing it out of there.

Argh.

His words rumbled inside her chest, tapping at her heart.

I've got you. You're safe.

She grazed her cheek, sure she could still feel his breath against her skin. The way the warmth of his hand on hers had spiraled up her arm.

An involuntary shudder rolled down her spine.

But…that was over now. Her little airplane fantasy man was gone, probably to see his runway model girlfriend, while she was almost at her hotel to promote this Christmas fair. *That* was what she needed to focus on—her job.

She pulled out her phone and frowned at two missed calls from Nate. He was her best friend's brother, but really, he was like a brother to her too. His family had basically let her grow up at their house when her own mother couldn't have cared less.

Why was he calling?

She tried returning the call but wasn't surprised when it went straight to voicemail. The man was a Navy SEAL. Which again begged the question—why was he calling?

Quickly, she sent a message to her best friend, Andi.

Finley: Do you know why your brother's calling me?

Andi didn't reply, but that wasn't a surprise either. She worked as a family doctor in their hometown of Redwood, so her time was usually filled with back-to-back patients.

With a sigh, she turned back to the window, the white of the snow causing a smile to tug at the corners of her lips. God, she loved Christmas. The excitement in the air. The songs that made her heart feel light. And of course the eggnog—that was an all-time favorite.

It was Thursday, just over a week away from Christmas next Saturday. And she got to spend it here, in Ontario, Canada. Gah, she was excited.

When the driver pulled off the road, she looked up at the multistory resort, her heart doing a little skip. As her social media following had grown, the jobs she'd been employed to market had become bigger, with more money being invested in *her*.

This was her biggest job yet, and with the best perks. A two-week stay at a ski resort over Christmas while she promoted a Christmas fair? Yes, please.

She climbed out, thanking her driver when he handed her the two bags and pulling one over her shoulder. Then, with a long inhale, she grabbed the handle of her other bag and rolled it toward the entrance, declining the help of the concierge.

The hotel's large open foyer was warm and welcoming. A huge fireplace sat to the right of the space, with couches scattered around the area. They looked so soft and plush, she just wanted to sink right into them. A couple snuggled by the fire, drinking from mugs topped with whipped cream, and her heart gave an excited little skip.

Yep, she was definitely going to enjoy this trip.

The door opened behind her, and she bit back a curse as she realized she was blocking the entrance.

She shuffled to the side. "Sorry, I'm in your—" The words died on her lips.

Holy shit…it was Nixon.

"What are you doing here?" The question was out before she could pull it back or idiot-proof it.

He lifted a brow. "I'm staying here, Finley."

It was the second time he'd said her name, and just like the first, every fine hair on her arms stood on end.

She swallowed. "Oh."

That was all she said. Oh…it barely qualified as a word. *Dammit, Finley.*

He held out a hand toward the check-in counter. "After you."

Her mouth opened and closed before she finally just nodded and stepped toward the desk.

"Finley Dunkley, checking in," she said quickly, drumming her fingers on the desk, using every ounce of self-restraint to not glance over her shoulder at the man behind her. It was hard. Listening to and processing the woman's words as she checked in was also hard.

She'd just signed the check-in form when she finally gave in and peeked over her shoulder. His gaze collided with hers and her breath caught.

Oh God.

"Here's your room card, Miss Dunkley."

She pulled her gaze away. "Thank you."

"You're welcome. Please let me know if there's anything else I can help you with."

She smiled at the woman, then turned and gave Nixon a tight let's-not-run-into-each-other-again smile before heading toward the elevator. She was halfway there when a text came through.

Andi: I'm sorry. Please don't hate me.

She stopped. Sorry? What was her best friend sorry about?

Then her phone rang, Nate's name popping up on the screen.

She lifted the cell to her ear, her heart thumping a bit faster. "Hey, Nate. Is everything okay?" Had something happened? God, was it their father? His heart wasn't doing great. Was it something to do with that?

"Hey, Fin." Nate's deep, familiar voice didn't sound stressed, so she relaxed a little. "I just wanted to check in that everything's okay with the bodyguard."

Her muscles froze, confusion swirling inside her. "Bodyguard?"

There was a short pause. "Andi told me she'd speak to you once you landed."

"Uh, no. She texted that she was sorry, but that's it."

"Oh, Jesus. Okay. She told me she'd speak to you, but I guess she's leaving that to me."

Unease coiled in her belly. "Nate…what's going on?"

"She mentioned that some asshole's been commenting on your social media posts, saying that you're theirs. That you'll meet at Christmas."

She scrubbed a hand over her face. "Nate, it's nothing. Just a stupid follower trying to get a rise out of me."

"She told me something was left at your door last week."

Her skin chilled at the memory, and it took her a moment to get the words out. "Yes. Mistletoe and a note saying they can't wait to meet me." Her pulse picked up. She hadn't felt safe in her home since.

"Finley. This is serious, and you should have told me."

"There have been no threats to actually hurt me—"

"It doesn't matter. A gift was left *at your front door*. They have your address. They know who you are and where you live. And they've escalated from social media comments to gifts. You don't want them to escalate more."

She swallowed. It was all true. "Nate, I still don't need—"

"This is nonnegotiable, Fin. You're family, even if we're not blood related. And I protect my family."

Some of the anger bled away at his words. How the heck was she supposed to argue with that? "Okay, let's say I go along with this little plan—"

"You *are* going along with it."

"Who is my…bodyguard?" God, that sounded strange on her lips.

"You should have already met him."

She frowned, her tummy doing a little roll as Nate continued.

"He's an old SEAL friend of mine who now works in security. After you told me your seat number, I booked him a seat next to you on the plane."

She gasped, her gaze lifting to Nixon at the counter.

"His name's Nixon Reid, and he's the best."

CHAPTER 4

"No. Absolutely not. If you wanted me to go along with this, I should have at least been part of the bodyguard decision process."

The corners of Nixon's mouth twitched. If the woman was trying to be quiet, she was doing a shit job of it. Her words were shouted whispers.

A part of him wanted to be offended at her insinuation that, had she made the decision, she wouldn't have chosen *him*. But then, she didn't really know him.

"Here's your room card, Mr. Reid. Please let us know if there's anything else you need."

He smiled at the woman, lifting the key card from the counter. "Thank you."

"No." Finley growled the word, hanging up the phone and shoving it into her pocket.

He was just heading toward the elevator when she spun toward him and blocked his way. Frustration darkened her brown eyes, and her fists slammed to her hips. The woman came to his shoulders and reminded him of an angry chipmunk.

"You knew."

It didn't seem to be a question, but he answered it anyway. "I did."

The anger darkened, her knuckles whitening. "Why on earth didn't you say anything?"

"Nate asked me not to until he gave me the all clear that you were told."

She huffed, her cheeks reddening. "Well, I'm sorry you flew all this way for nothing, but your job is canceled." She spun around, grabbing the handle of her bag and rolling it forward. He got three steps in behind her before she peeked a look over her shoulder, then turned on him again. "What are you doing?"

"Going to my room."

"No. You need to go home."

He laughed. "Even if I did get confirmation from Nate that this job was terminated, I doubt I'd get a flight out tonight."

The line in her brow deepened, like the truth in that statement only frustrated her further.

A couple walked past, eyeing them closely.

Nixon lowered his voice. "Maybe we should have this conversation in one of our rooms."

Her jaw tightened, and it took a moment for her to respond. "Fine. But you'll just be told the same thing."

Finley spun again and marched toward the elevator before jamming her finger on the button so hard he thought she'd dislocate something. When the doors opened and he followed her inside, she was all he could smell. That sweet floral scent again. Because being surrounded by it for the two-hour flight hadn't been enough.

When the doors opened on the fifth floor and he followed her out, she eyed him suspiciously. She stopped halfway down the hall, and he stopped at the door beside hers.

"Really? Your room's right beside mine?" She swiped her card and moved inside her room.

If she didn't like that, she *really* wouldn't like—

"You've got to be kidding me."

He stepped inside his room to find she'd opened the connecting door.

"I'm not angry at you. I'm angry at the situation. *Really* angry. Don't get comfortable. This isn't happening."

"You do realize I'm here to help you, right?"

"Nate and Andi should have been honest with me. And even though Nate told you not to, you still should have told me who you were on the plane."

She stepped back and closed the door before he could respond.

Dropping his bag on the bed, he looked around the large hotel room. There was a mini bar in the corner, a big TV opposite the bed, and a bathroom. He ignored all of it, grabbing his phone and calling Nate as he moved to the window.

His friend answered on the first ring. "I know what you're gonna say, Nix."

"This isn't gonna work." The man had been a friend for years, but there was a line, and protecting a fully grown woman who clearly didn't want his protection was it.

"Andi's calling her right now. She'll convince her."

The Christmas decorations at the front of the hotel made nausea crawl through his gut. "And if she can't?"

"She will. Finley knows she needs you. And we need her safe. She's family, and someone's targeting her."

He knew both those things. Nate considered the woman a sister, and the asshole who was harassing her was escalating.

"Just let Andi work her magic," Nate continued. "If anyone can turn Finley around, it's her."

Nixon blew out a breath. "I don't like this."

"I know. And I hate that I put you in this position. But you're the only guy I trust to keep her safe."

Nixon ran a hand over his face. Goddammit, how could he say no to that? "Fine."

"Thank you. Not only for staying, but for being there at this time of year. I know it's hard for you."

Understatement of the fucking century. "You'd do the same for me."

His friend didn't have an aversion to the holiday, but Nixon was sure if he called in a favor, Nate would be there in a second.

They'd been on the same SEAL team for years, covering each other's backs, saving each other more times than he could count. That forged a bond that could never be broken.

"I would," Nate said quietly. "Thank you. I'll let you know once they've spoken."

When Nixon hung up, he watched a couple of kids play in the snow in front of the hotel. A young boy and girl, probably siblings. Most people would smile at the sight. He didn't. It made him think of his own sister. A reminder he didn't need.

* * *

"It's not what you did, Andi, it's that you didn't tell me." Finley ran her fingers over the soft white duvet, frustration thrumming through her veins.

Nixon knew. The entire flight, the man had known exactly who she was and had said nothing. And more than that, Andi had gone behind her back, told Nate about this follower of hers, then she and Nate had decided she needed protection without her consultation.

"I know, Finley. I'm really sorry. It just all happened really quickly. You only told me about the mistletoe that was left on your doorstep a day before you left. I was worried because mistletoe is synonymous with Christmas, and you'd just announced to your followers that you're attending this Christmas fair. I told Nate, and he organized protection. By the time I knew what was going on, you were a few hours from boarding your flight and I knew you got anxious on planes, so...I don't know…I guess I figured it would be easier for everyone to ask for your forgiveness after it was done."

"Easier for who, Andi?"

Her friend groaned. "I know. I hate myself for it. But I love you. And Nate loves you. It's why we did this."

God, how could she be mad at her best friend after that?

"I didn't know Nate would go the extra mile and make sure the guy would be sitting right next to you," Andi added.

She drew a circle on the bed, sighing. "I just feel embarrassed that I didn't know."

"I'm sorry, Fin. I really am. But please don't send him away. You've had weird followers before, but this guy feels different. God, he found your *address*."

It was true. The mistletoe showing up at her home had scared her. "Was he just hired for this trip?"

"At the moment."

She sucked in a long breath and blew it out before asking, "What do you know about Nixon?"

"Not much. Just that he was a SEAL and served with Nate. He now works as a bodyguard. And he's the best."

She nibbled her bottom lip, eyeing the connecting door, still hating that it was there. "I could have told you that just by looking at him. He's a million feet tall and all muscle."

"So he's cute?" Andi whispered, even though no one else would be able to hear.

Finley rolled her eyes. "He's a former SEAL…*cute* is not a word I would use to describe the man."

Big. Rugged. Intense. They all felt a lot more fitting.

"I fell asleep on his shoulder," Finley whispered.

"Oh my gosh, you didn't…"

Her friend sounded far too excited. And despite everything, she laughed. "I did. Again, it was embarrassing."

A knock at the door had her gaze shooting up. "I have to go."

"Does this mean you're accepting the protection?"

"For this trip. Then, together, we discuss what we do after." She swallowed. "And I do appreciate you and Nate looking out for me. But next time, you talk to me first. Even if I'm five minutes from stepping on a plane."

"Deal. And I should tell you that Erik knows as well. I told him after Nate, and he was going to go in all guns blazing with some paid protection, but Nate beat him to it."

Finley rolled her eyes. She wasn't as close to Andi's oldest brother, Erik. He was the most intense of the Hunter siblings, but she still considered him family. "So if I don't want your overprotective brothers to move in on my life, I shouldn't tell you things?"

"Afraid so, Fin."

She shook her head. "Okay, I've got to go. But thank you for looking out for me."

"Always. Keep me updated and stay safe."

When she hung up, she eyed the door like it was a bomb about to detonate. Then, slowly, she rose to her feet and moved over to it. When she pulled it open, the sight of Nixon almost stole her breath. Why did he have to be so tall and toned and bronzed?

"Everything okay?" he asked in his too-sexy-for-her-own-good voice.

She swallowed. "Yes. I'm still frustrated that no one told me who you were on the plane. But I understand...kind of."

"Good. Should we run through security detail?"

She frowned. "I thought you'd just follow me from a distance."

He stepped into her room, taking up all the space. "Yes. I'll trail you. But I need to know where you're going and what you're doing. I'd also like to see all communication this person's had with you. Nate shared what he knew, but he said there's more."

A shudder raced down her spine at the memory. She lifted her phone and went into the photos she'd saved—screenshots of every comment from this guy.

"It started about six months ago. He'd leave comments on my TikTok and Instagram posts. A few on my YouTube videos. At first, I thought nothing of them. I have a lot of followers on my platforms, and it's not unusual to get inappropriate comments here and there. Usually, I just block the account and move on. But this person keeps creating new accounts and leaving new comments."

Nixon's brows slashed together. "How do you know it's always him?"

"He signs off 'KJ' at the end of each message." She handed him the phone and watched as his muscles visibly bunched while he read the posts.

She didn't need to look over his shoulder to know what they said.

You're so beautiful. You make my heart race. KJ.

I can't wait to meet you. KJ.

We're gonna be so perfect together. KJ.

And then the guy had started commenting about Christmas. About how it was his favorite time of the year. About how special it would be to meet on the holiday.

She rubbed her arms in an attempt to ward off a sudden chill.

When a low growl sounded from Nixon, she looked up to see every part of him had become...harder. Darker.

"And he left you mistletoe on your doorstep," he said, the words less a question and more a confirmation.

"Yes. And a note saying he couldn't wait to meet me." She swallowed.

The anger in his eyes was so distinct, she almost felt it. "Why are you still posting then? Why are you here at all?"

She blinked. "This is my *job*. I market social events and get the word out to my followers."

"This is your *life*, Finley. The asshole's told you he wants you. That Christmas is his target date to meet up. The second you post about this event, he'll know you're here."

Anger straightened her spine. "I've already posted that I'm coming here. And I will not be forced into hiding by this asshole. This is the biggest job I've gotten to date. My business is important to me, and I *will* complete the jobs I've committed to."

"Will you still be saying that if this asshole gets his hands on you?"

Fear fluttered in her belly, but she made sure not to show it. "He won't. Besides, that's why you're here, isn't it? To make sure that doesn't happen?"

He stepped forward, towering over her. "Nate and I can organize a safe house for you. Somewhere no one will be able to find you."

"No. And it's not your job to advise me on life decisions." She tried to step away, but he grabbed her wrist, tugging her back. The touch singed her skin, burning her.

He lowered his head. "Part of my job as a bodyguard *is* to advise you. I will do my job and protect you, but I think you being here is a stupid decision."

Oh, this man...one minute whispering sweet things into her ear about being safe with him, and the next telling her she was stupid. "You're not the first person to call me stupid. You're also not the first person I'm choosing not to listen to."

CHAPTER 5

*N*ixon knocked on the connecting door between his and Finley's rooms. It had taken him too damn long to get to sleep last night, but then, that wasn't a surprise. At this time of year, he barely slept at all.

The door opened, and every goddamn muscle in his body tightened. Fuck, she was beautiful. She wore a black beanie and jacket over a pale pink shirt. It was paired with leggings that were so tight they were like a second skin.

"Hey." She gave him a small smile, swinging a bag over her shoulder. "Ready to go?"

No. Because this woman made all the put-together parts of him tug apart at the seams. And that made him almost dread spending time with her.

He cleared his throat. "Yeah. You?"

"Yep, got all my gear."

The back of his teeth ground together. A part of him understood that this was her job and what she had to do, but the other part of him, the part that had seen the depth of ugly in this world, wanted to grab that goddamn gear and throw it away. She'd use it to post about her life for the world to see. It was her connection to this asshole who was stalking her.

She slipped past him into his room, and he got a blast of that now-familiar sweet scent.

Fuck, Nate owed him for this.

He followed her into the hall, then the elevator. "So, the fair's closed today and you'll just be meeting the organizers, right?"

"That's right. I've been communicating with Beth, and she's lovely. She's going to show me around today, then I can take some footage for a video I'll put together tonight."

Another ground of his goddamn teeth. "No posting where you're staying, though."

She rolled her eyes like he'd just told her not to swim in the icy lake. "I'm not being paid by the resort. I'm being paid by the Winter Wonderland organizers, so that's what I'll post."

When the elevator stopped and a middle-aged man stepped in, his gaze roamed over Finley's chest, then her thighs. Nixon narrowed his eyes on the guy, and the second their gazes caught, the man's eyes widened, and he looked away.

When the elevator stopped at the lobby, Nixon placed a hand on the small of Finley's back and led her out to his rental car. The fair was only five minutes from the resort. Another thing he fucking hated. If the scumbag wanted to know where she was staying, this was the closest place. The only thing that made him feel slightly better was the fact that the resort was big, which meant even if he assumed she was here, it would be hell to figure out which room she was in.

He opened Finley's door and waited for her to climb in.

She smiled at him. "Looks like chivalry isn't dead. Thank you."

When she brushed against his side, his gut tightened. Why did this woman's touch affect him so much?

As he walked around the vehicle, he scanned the parking lot, searching for anyone's lingering stare. There were none. Good.

Once they were driving, Finley sighed. "Don't you love this time of year?"

The only reason he didn't tense at her words was years of practice. He didn't answer, but then, he didn't need to because she didn't seem to notice.

"And being here in Fallen Ridge almost feels magical, what with the snow and festivities,"

she continued. "And God, I'm excited for the eggnog."

He frowned. "Eggnog?"

"Yeah. It's a Christmas obsession of mine. Some like hot cocoa, some cider. I'm definitely an eggnog girl. When I'm not drinking it, I dream about the stuff."

"You dream about eggnog?" Who the hell dreamed about eggnog?

She turned in her seat a bit to look at him. "Don't tell me you don't like it?"

"I don't like it."

She gasped like he'd just said he kidnapped puppies as a hobby.

When her gaze continued to sit on him, he shot her a glance. "What?"

"I just don't know how you and Nate are friends. He *loves* eggnog. Not to mention he smiles a lot more than you."

His lips twitched. "There's more to friendship than eggnog and smiles."

She cocked her head. "You served together, right?"

The smile slipped from his face as the memories of his time as a SEAL came back to him. Some good. Some so fucking hard they slammed into his gut like a physical blow. "We did. It created a brotherhood like none other."

She swallowed. "I hated it when he became a SEAL. I should have been used to it because his brother Erik was a Marine. But I hated that they joined the military at all. It's so dangerous. I was scared for them. I'm *still* scared for Nate."

"He's good at what he does. He can look after himself."

She nodded. "I know. It's still dangerous, though. Why'd you leave the military?"

"I was thinking about it for a while. I was being sent out on back-to-back tours and started to feel like there was no end in sight. While it feels good to know you're making a difference, it also wears you to the bone." He tightened his fingers around the wheel. "There's a lot of death in that line of work. The need to get out grew stronger, so when a friend offered me a position in his security business as a bodyguard, I took it."

When Finley touched his arm, his muscles rippled beneath her fingertips. "Thank you for your service."

He turned to look at her again, seeing true gratitude in her soft brown eyes. He dipped his chin.

When they pulled in at the venue, a vein throbbed in his temple at the sight of decorated Christmas trees. The Christmas garlands and big inflatable Santas. He ignored them all and climbed out of the car. He kept his head on a swivel as he walked to her door and tugged it open.

Just beyond the lot was a bridge over an iced lake. On the other side was a large warehouse-type building to the left, and a trailer on the right. Farther down, there were more paths with signs for things like ice-skating and snowman building.

What he hated the most was the woods that bordered the entire area. Too many places to hide.

Once they were over the bridge, the door to the trailer opened and a woman stepped out, her mouth curving into a smile when she saw them. She had long red hair that hit about midback and green eyes.

The woman stopped in front of them and held out her hand. "Finley. I recognize you from your platforms. I'm Beth, the organizer who's been inundating you with emails."

Finley shook her hand. "It's nice to finally put a face to the name."

"I am so glad you're here. Just the TikTok you posted a week ago to announce you were coming got this event so much traction."

"It went semi-viral, which is exactly what we want."

The woman's attention shifted to Nixon, and Finley glanced up at him. "Sorry, this is my…friend, Nixon. He'll be taking a lot of the footage for me."

The fuck? They'd already gotten their stories straight that he was her assistant, but he'd thought they'd at least be telling the organizer what was going on.

He narrowed his eyes at Finley to see her giving him a don't-you-dare-tell-her-the-truth glare. His jaw clicked and he shook the woman's hand. "Nice to meet you."

"You too. Got to say, you look more like a bodyguard than an assistant."

Finley laughed. The sound was light and airy and felt like a punch to the chest. "Let's not stroke his ego."

Beth lifted a shoulder. "You could always pop him into some of the footage? I think he'd get you some views."

That was never happening. And why were they talking about him like he wasn't standing right fucking here?

"Don't tempt me," Finley said.

Beth laughed. "All right, time for the tour. The trailer is where I disappear to do all the behind-the-scenes organizing, including contacting social media gurus like you to promote the fair."

She turned toward the building to their left. "The warehouse isn't being used. It's an old office building and kind of rundown. It would have taken too much time to clean, so we're just keeping it locked up. I've been using it as a storage area." The woman led them down a path, and they followed her to more trailers. "These are the food outlets. There's also an indoor area we've set up a bit farther down. The drinks are to die for. Trust me when I tell you, you need to get a hot cocoa with cream and a cherry."

"Oh my gosh, you're talking straight to my stomach, Beth."

They kept moving, and the woman showed them the ice-skating rink, a tobogganing hill, a horse-and-sleigh station—although there were no horses in sight today—and the snowman-building area.

Nixon barely looked at the events themselves, instead keeping his gaze on the trees around them. All the places someone could hide. And starting tomorrow, this place would be crawling with people.

They'd just returned to the tobogganing hill when Beth received a call and stepped away to answer. Finley turned to him, frustration darkening her features. "You could try to smile."

"Why would I do that?"

"Because it's Christmas and this place is beautiful."

"I hate Christmas."

Her jaw dropped, and for a moment she was silent, as if trying to decipher if he was messing with her or not.

Her voice lowered as though she was scared someone would hear her. "You hate Christmas? No one hates Christmas."

Countless people hated Christmas. "I do."

"Why? Christmas is about family and fun and celebration."

The muscles in his forearms twitched. Not for him. It had stopped being all of that a long damn time ago.

When he didn't respond, she looked like she wanted to push but then shook her head. "Okay, if you're not gonna smile for Christmas, then smile because you're supposed to be my assistant."

"I'm not your assistant. I'm your bodyguard."

Finley rolled her eyes. "Beth doesn't know that."

"Why not? She's the event organizer. Shouldn't she know you have a stalker?"

"I can't tell her I have someone sending me messages that are so creepy I need protection! I need to do a great job marketing this event so I get booked again."

Before he could respond, Beth returned, an apologetic look

on her face. "I'm sorry, we have an emergency with the ice. Is it okay if I leave you both to it? Explore as much as you want and take any footage you need."

The smile returned to Finley's face, but there was a hint of strain in her eyes. "Not a problem. Thank you for showing us around, Beth. I'll take some footage and create a post tonight."

"Thank you."

The woman disappeared, and Finley held out her phone. "Could you take a video for me?"

"No."

Her gaze swung to him. "Nixon—"

"I'm here to protect you, not be your videographer."

There was another roll of her eyes. His lips twitched. He was getting used to them.

"Fine. I'll do it myself." She held the phone out in front of her, face transforming with a smile so radiant he forgot to breathe for a moment. Then she started recording herself as she walked around the event grounds.

He was fucking transfixed. By her smile. The way her eyes lit with excitement as she spoke.

This was why people followed her. God, he could barely take his eyes off her.

She only stopped when she reached the bridge, pausing beside the water. She ended the video and snapped a photo of herself before typing something on her phone.

When he peered over her shoulder and saw she was posting the photo online, he reached over and snatched the phone out of her hand.

Finley gasped and spun. "What the hell?"

* * *

First, the man had been a grump all day. Now he was taking her damn phone?

"You don't post until you've left the location."

"Excuse me?" Okay, this guy was really getting on her last nerve. "First of all, you don't tell me what to do. Second, everyone knows I'm here, and we're gonna leave in a few minutes."

"I don't care. You don't post until we're gone. That's my rule."

She lifted a brow. So this guy thought he was the damn rulemaker now? "*Your* rule?"

"Yes."

Just…yes?

Her eyes narrowed as she held out her hand. "Give it to me."

"No."

If there was ever a definition of jackass, it would be this guy. "Nixon—"

"You can have it when you tell me you won't post right now."

"I won't post right now." The answer came quickly. Maybe too quickly, because this time *his* eyes narrowed.

"I don't believe you."

Goddammit. She tried to grab her phone, but he swiped his hand away.

"Okay, I'm trying to not lose my shit on you, but you're making it really hard." She was right on the damn edge.

"I'm not giving it to you so you can tell the world where you are," he growled.

"Give it back, *now.*"

She reached for the phone again. Again, he held his hand back.

Anger boiled in her belly, to the point she lost all sanity and lunged. A full-body lunge that sent her flying forward. Except Nixon turned his body, and instead of hitting him, she fell toward the iced-over water beneath the bridge.

Her stomach dropped, the air whipping from her lungs. She was a second from hitting the hard surface when strong fingers wrapped around her wrist and tugged her to the side.

Then they were *both* off balance, and she kept falling, hitting snow, Nixon catching himself on his hands above her.

Her breath snagged, her eyes flashing up to see Nixon covering her. Surrounding her.

She told herself to breathe. To move the air through her lungs. But his heat, his deep masculine scent, was everywhere…and it suffocated her. He was so close, she saw every intricate detail of his face. The day-old stubble. The specks of black in his brown eyes.

For a moment, their gazes clashed, and she wasn't sure if he was breathing either.

"Are you okay?" His breath brushed her face as he spoke, whispers of heat across her skin.

"Yes." The reply was so quiet that she wasn't sure if it had actually touched air or if she'd just mouthed the word.

He stared at her, an odd expression in his eyes. Almost involuntarily, her gaze shifted to his mouth. When she looked up again, his eyes were darker.

For a split second, she thought he might close the distance between them and kiss her. It made her lips tingle and her belly do a funny little flip.

Suddenly, he was on his feet and just like that, the spell broke.

He reached down, wrapped his fingers around her wrist, and tugged her up. His hand was warm and sent sparks of awareness down her arm.

With one hand on the back of hers, he set her phone in her palm. "Don't post shit while you're in the location." His words were short and clipped. "Let's go."

Then he turned and walked away, while she was left wondering what the hell had just happened.

CHAPTER 6

$\mathcal{N}$ixon counted out his push-ups, forcing his body to move while ignoring the tremble of his arms and the groan of his muscles.

He'd been working out so long that sweat beaded on his bare chest. But he needed to keep moving. He needed to chase the feeling of Finley's body under his out of his damn mind. The soft curves of her hips. The way her eyes had darkened before shifting to his mouth.

Fuck. He'd only met the woman yesterday—she shouldn't have such a goddamn effect on him.

He didn't date women under his protection. Even if it wasn't a company policy, it would be *his* rule. What kind of an asshole hit on women they looked after?

More than that, though, he didn't date. Never had.

He counted three more push-ups before rolling to his back and starting on sit-ups.

Every so often, he heard Finley in the room beside his. Moving around. Typing on a computer.

Notes were scattered across his bed. Printouts he'd made of every comment the asshole had posted on her socials. At the start, the comments had been innocent enough. Compliments about her looks. Her smile. Her voice. But they'd escalated quickly, shifting to comments about looking forward to meeting her. Touching her. About Finley belonging to him.

Nixon bit back a curse.

Memories of another asshole popped into his mind. Of his sister's ex. The way *his* messages became more frequent. More vile. Telling her that she was his. That they belonged together.

He'd only been a teenager then. He hadn't understood what those messages could escalate into. None of his family had.

He flipped onto his stomach and started on one-handed push-ups, welcoming the ache to his limbs.

There were too many parallels between his sister's stalker and this case, and it was messing with his head.

When he heard Finley's voice in the room next door, he paused to determine if she had a visitor. Then he heard her say Andi's name, and he continued.

She was talking on the phone. Good. He'd told the woman not to answer the door unless he was there, but at this point, he wasn't sure what the hell she would listen to and what she wouldn't. She was fighting him on every goddamn thing, and he didn't like it. He was used to the people he protected listening to him. *Wanting* his help.

When his phone rang, he rose to his feet, seeing it was his boss, Jacob.

He pressed the phone to his ear. "Hey."

"Hey, Nix. Everything going okay over there?"

He could have laughed. Depended on what the man meant by *okay*. "It's fine. The asshole hasn't shown his face yet, and there have been no messages. But she's posting her first video tonight. She might have already done it. So we'll see."

"Good to hear it's all been quiet." There was a small pause. "You doing okay?"

A muscle in his jaw clenched. Jacob was more a friend than a boss, and he knew exactly what Nixon had been through and where his hatred of Christmas stemmed from. "Not really, but I'm managing. And I'm making sure my client's safe."

That was his priority. That was what he was focusing on.

"I know you're keeping her safe. You're the best guy I have. But if you need someone else to swap with you—"

"No. I'm fine." When he committed to a job, he made sure to see it through. Plus, Nate had wanted *him* because he trusted him. He wasn't going to let his friend down.

Jacob sighed. "Okay. Call if you need anything."

"Will do."

Nixon was just ending the call when a scream sounded from Finley's room.

He dropped the cell to the bed, grabbed his Glock from the bedside drawer and ran through the connecting door, adrenaline pumping through his veins.

His feet slammed to a stop at the sight of Finley, standing beside the bed in a lacy black bra and panties.

She screamed again, phone dropping from her hand to the floor as she grabbed at the bedspread and tugged it up to cover her body. "What the hell, Nixon?"

He shot his gaze around the room. When nothing looked out of place, he swung his attention back to her. "You screamed. I thought someone was in here."

"No! I'm on the phone with Andi and she told me some good news, you psycho." With a huff, she lifted the cell to her ear. "I have to call you back."

He scowled. "Do you always wear just your underwear when you talk to your friends on the phone?"

Her eyes narrowed. "I was changing so I could go for a run. Can you at least turn around so I can finish getting dressed?"

He turned, and at the sound of material moving over her body, the muscles in his forearms tightened and he clenched his fists. "Are you going to the gym here in the resort?"

"No. I like to run outside."

What the hell? "It's pretty cold out there." Not to mention there was snow everywhere.

"I know. I like to run in the cold. I get warm quickly, and there's a path the hotel keeps clear of snow." Another few seconds passed. "Okay, you can turn now."

He turned around to find her wearing leggings and a grey sweatshirt.

She cocked her head. "Why are you shirtless and sweaty?"

"I was working out."

"Oh." She swallowed, her gaze roaming down his chest, then back up. His muscles locked at the way her gaze moved over his body. At the way he *liked* how her gaze moved over his body. "Well…I'm guessing you'd like to come with me."

How was that even a question? "Yes."

She sighed and lifted her phone again, touching the screen. "I thought so—"

Her eyes locked on the device. When the color drained from her face, he was across the room in a second, slipping the cell from her fingers.

His gaze zeroed in on the comment, a rage-filled breath hissing from between his teeth. It was a comment on the newest Instagram video of her at the Christmas fair.

I can't wait to meet you, my love. Soon. KJ.

* * *

FINLEY'S FEET pounded the pavement, her arms pumping back and forth. She'd been running for so long that her lungs ached and her skin had long stopped feeling the cold. But it wasn't enough. She wanted to move faster. To outrun every twisted emotion that chased her. Hounded her.

The anger. The frustration. And the fear… God, she *hated* the fear. There was no part of her that should be allowing this man to scare her with his words. That was what he *wanted*. He wanted to affect her. To make her vividly aware that he was nearby at all times.

He didn't deserve that kind of validation.

She pushed herself to move faster, memories of the mistletoe and note on her porch coming back to her again. Of the terror that had raced through her body at the realization this KJ person had somehow gotten her address. That he could have been watching her not only opening the note but every moment before and after.

She'd gone straight to a hotel at the time.

Her belly cramped and she sped up, air now sawing in and out of her chest.

Why couldn't this asshole just leave her alone? Let her build her business in peace! She hadn't been born into privilege. She'd worked her way up to where she was today all on her own. And now this person was messing with her. Threatening everything.

She rounded a curve, her gaze catching on a man who sat by the lake, phone to his ear. She couldn't help the thud of her heart, and God, even that made her angry. That she couldn't look at a person, a random man she was passing, without wondering if it was *him*.

She was still pushing herself to run too fast, the air whooshing in and out of her chest, when strong fingers wrapped around her arm. "Finley."

She finally stopped and turned, her chest heaving as she glanced at Nixon. He'd been behind her the entire time, but while she could barely get a breath, his chest was hardly moving.

He took a small step toward her. "You need to slow down."

As if proving his point, her breaths shortened and black dots hedged her vision. She'd pushed herself too hard, and now she was paying the price.

Nixon's brows furrowed and his fingers wrapped around her hips. "Breathe, Finley. In and out."

His chest rose as he inhaled a long, exaggerated breath. She followed, doing the same as she forced air into her lungs. When he released the air in his lungs, she did too. With each breath, she never took her eyes off him. His fingers felt strong on her hips. Like they were all that kept her from falling.

One of those hands rose to her cheek, and when he spoke, his voice was soft. "Are you okay?"

It was only the gentleness of his voice, so different from his usual hardness, that had her wanting to give him the truth instead of an easy lie. "No. Who is he? Why is he doing this?"

His biceps twitched. "There are assholes in the world who don't need much reason to harass and hurt others."

She swallowed and shook her head. "I know that putting my life out there on social media leaves me open to this kind of stuff, but—"

"That doesn't make this okay. And it doesn't mean you deserve it."

She swallowed. "I'm scared."

She'd never admitted that out loud, but it was true. Since that mistletoe had reached her front door, she'd been terrified of this person, knowing that their presence wasn't merely online.

For a moment, she regretted her honesty because Nixon might use it to push her to go home again. But she couldn't do that either. This was her business. Her job. And she was just as scared about losing that.

Nixon's eyes hardened and he stepped closer, eliminating any space between them. "Nothing is going to happen to you. I won't allow it. You're safe with me."

Safe...he'd told her the same thing on the plane. And just like then, the words flowed through her limbs, taking root deep inside her chest. She *did* feel safe with him. A man she barely knew. A man she'd fought with more than she'd befriended. Yet he made her believe that he would protect her. And it wasn't just his size or his history as a Navy SEAL. It was the confidence that coated his words when he said them. The belief in his eyes.

"Thank you," she whispered.

Then, before she could stop herself, or even really understand what she was doing, she wrapped her arms around his waist and hugged him.

For a single heartbeat, he was still. So still that she was about to step back, when his arms came around her and tugged her closer. His hug was tight and warm, and it made the last trickles of unease and dread leave her limbs as she sank deeper into the sanctuary that was Nixon.

CHAPTER 7

Nixon's fingers were tight around the wheel. Today was the first day the fair was open to the public. That, along with it being a Saturday the week before Christmas, meant there'd be a lot of damn people. People who could be this KJ asshole and a threat to Finley.

He shot a quick glance her way to see her eyes on the passenger-side window. When they'd returned to the hotel last night, they'd ordered room service and eaten together. It was the quietest Finley had been so far.

Because she felt the shift between them? Because she was as fucking confused by it as he was?

When she'd hugged him yesterday, something had shifted in his chest, and his vow to protect her had only been cemented further.

Holding her had felt good. *Right*. And it also made him want to burn down the fucking world to find and stop this asshole who was targeting her.

After pulling into the parking lot, he climbed out of the car and walked around to the other side to help Finley out. He placed a hand on the small of her back and led her toward the entrance, not missing her slight misstep at his touch. The way her gaze fluttered up to his before quickly shifting away.

As they crossed the bridge, Nixon fought like hell to not look at the place where they'd fallen yesterday. It was a damn effort.

"What's the plan today?" he asked gruffly.

"Snowman building." She lifted a shoulder. "It's a fun, easy first activity with little chance of injury."

He nodded and took the marked path. When two girls approached, their eyes only for Finley, he angled his body in front of hers.

The taller girl's brows flickered, and she took a small step back. "Sorry. I just wanted to see if I could get a photo with Finley." Her gaze shifted to Finley. "We've been following you on your channels for a while and love your content!"

Finley touched his arm, stepping up beside him. "Of course. I'm sure my *assistant* here wouldn't mind taking the photo." She narrowed her eyes, clarifying with a single look what she thought of his protective move. There was also the hint of a threat there in case he said no.

He *wanted* to say no. He didn't. He slipped the phone from the girl's hand and took a quick photo of the three of them before handing it back to her.

The girl's lips parted. "Oh, could you take a couple in case—"

"No."

If looks could kill, Finley's would be slashing into his chest right now. She shifted her attention back to the girl, her smile easy. "Sorry. He hasn't had his morning coffee. If the photo isn't great, just come find me for another."

Both girls smiled and nodded before heading off.

Finley grabbed his arm and tugged him close. "You need to be nice."

"I told you I'm not your assistant, and I'm certainly not your photographer."

She shook her head. "I know you're really good at this I-hate-

Christmas thing, but try to loosen up. Don't all these smiling, happy people make *you* happy?"

"No." *Crowds* while he was protecting someone meant multiple threats.

She sighed as she moved to the snowman-making area of the fair. She grabbed a shovel from one of several barrels full of them, then all but jammed it into his hands. Then she lifted a bucket of supplies that contained a carrot, sticks and rocks, and a beanie.

An ache started behind his temple. Christmas...it fucking surrounded him.

Finley led him to a mound of snow near the edge of the area and dropped the bucket. "Are you at least going to help me make a snowman?"

He wanted to say no, but then he'd feel like a total asshole, and it would take her twice as long to finish. The quicker she was done, the quicker they could leave. "I'll help you. But if you're gonna film, make sure I'm not in it."

Excitement lit her eyes. "Deal."

Damn, just the sight of her smile made him want to do more to get another one.

She set up her tripod, angling the phone so it was just her in the shot, then they started building the snowman.

It didn't take him long to realize how bad he was at it. He mostly shoveled more snow onto the mound, but that was because anytime he tried to shape the body, Finley grimaced and redid his work.

She talked the entire time. About her life in Redwood. About the Hunter family and everything they'd done for her. He noticed she barely mentioned her own mother and father. In fact, she seemed very careful to avoid mentioning her family at all.

Nate had given him the CliffsNotes. Her father had died when she was young. She'd lived with her mother, but they didn't get along so she'd moved out the second she turned eighteen.

Before that, she'd spent large chunks of her time at the Hunters' home.

When the snowman's body was formed, Finley grabbed the carrot and rocks and pushed them into the snowman to build a face. Then she passed him the beanie.

"Last part's yours."

He slipped the hat from her fingers and set it on the snowman's head.

Finished. Good.

He turned back to look at Finley, and his chest squeezed. She beamed at him, her smile so radiant, every part of her lit up. "We did it!"

"We did."

"Only took us…" She looked down at her phone. "Holy crap, it took us an hour and a half."

He glanced at his own watch. Damn, she was right. Where had that time gone? And why did he suddenly wish they could linger? "Good work."

If possible, her smile got wider. Then she threw her arms around him for the second time in two days. Just like yesterday, the affection surprised the shit out of him. He wasn't a hugger. Hell, he'd barely hugged another person in his entire adult life.

Today, he was a bit quicker at pulling himself out of his shock and wrapping his arms around her. Because he *wanted* to hug her. To hold her.

God, she was soft. Her skin. Her breath. Everything about her was his complete opposite, and he was drawn to all of it.

"Finley Dunkley?"

Nixon's gaze shifted to the man beside them.

Fuck, he'd been so consumed by her and the feel of her against him, he hadn't heard or seen the guy drawing close. As they separated, Nixon angled his body in front of Finley.

She smiled at the guy. "Yes?"

"I'm Rad, Beth's cousin and the other event coordinator here."

Rad? What the fuck kind of name was Rad? And since when were there two event coordinators? In the notes he'd been given on the fair, only Beth's name was listed.

"Ah, yes. Beth told me about you. You take all the jobs she doesn't want, right?"

He laughed, and the sound grated on Nixon's skin. "Unfortunately. I'm usually the emergency guy when something's not going right."

Finley nodded. "A very important job." She looked up at Nixon. "This is my assistant, Nixon."

His teeth ground together at the fucking title. The guy dipped his head, a fraction of his smile slipping. The action was small, but Nixon saw it.

"Hi." The guy turned back to Finley. "I was hoping we could meet up and talk about the event."

"Sure. I'm free now."

"Actually, I have about a dozen fires to put out. I was thinking I could come by Copper Ski Resort this evening, and we could talk about it over a drink in the bar."

Fuck off. What, was this asshole trying to get into her pants? He looked at her like she was a fucking prize to be won.

"Oh, um… To talk about the event?"

Rad nodded. "Yes. I have some great content ideas I'd love you to film."

She nibbled her bottom lip.

Say no, Finley. Hell, tell him to fuck right off.

She didn't. She smiled and nodded. "Okay. Should we say eight in the resort bar?"

* * *

"You're not wearing that."

The smile slipped from Finley's lips. God, she'd only just

44

opened the connecting doors between their rooms, and he was already being a pain in her ass. "I am. I love this outfit."

She'd matched her tight black jeans with red heels and a spaghetti strap red top. Not to mention the jacket.

His jaw clenched, and when he spoke it was through gritted teeth. "The man will already be all over you. Don't you have a big, baggy top or something?"

She rolled her eyes, grabbing her clutch and stepping into his room. "It's a business meeting. And even if he *does* like the way I look—which I'm not saying he does or will—I'm not into him."

Rad was six foot, with short brown hair. Kind of cute in a clean-cut way, if you were into that kind of thing. She wasn't. For some reason, growly, rough-around-the-edges, dark-eyed men did it for her.

It was annoying.

She watched Nixon as they left his room and headed down the hall to the elevator. The man looked like he was carved from stone, he was so hard and tense. He wore a gray shirt, which pulled tightly against his sculpted muscles, and jeans that did nothing to hide his powerful thighs.

Yeah, the man was *all* power.

They stepped into the empty elevator, and when Nixon's stony silence continued, she touched his arm. "Hey. It will be a quick meeting about content, then we'll be back in our rooms."

"I'll believe that when I see it." The words were whispered under his breath, but Finley caught every one of them.

With a sigh, she waited for the doors to open, then walked through the resort. She stopped at the bar entrance. Holy crap, the place was classy. And romantic with its dim lighting, leather couches, and beige touches.

She spotted Rad immediately. He sat at the bar, drink in front of him. She moved forward, heels clicking against the marble floor. Before she could reach him, Nixon wrapped his fingers around her arm, causing her to pause.

He leaned down, his breath brushing her cheek as he whispered, "I'll be at the table beside the bar. Keep it professional."

Her brows flickered. He almost said it like a warning.

A part of her raged that he had no right to tell her to keep it professional. The other part of her, the part she would absolutely not admit to, *liked* the warning. As if maybe he didn't like her having a drink with another guy.

Before letting go, he grazed her bare skin with his thumb and a shudder rolled down her spine, tingling over her body. She sucked in a breath to steady herself before moving over to the bar.

"Hi, Rad."

The guy looked up, his eyes darkening. He didn't even try to hide the way his gaze roamed down to her breasts. And right now, she was kind of wishing she'd listened to Nixon's advice and changed into a big, baggy top.

Finally, his gaze rose. "Finley. You look gorgeous." He touched her elbow, urging her onto the stool beside his.

Unlike when Nixon touched her, this guy's hands on her felt wrong. She pulled away from his touch, lowering to a stool.

Rad called over the bartender before turning to her. "What would you like to drink? They do really good cocktails."

"I'm not much of a cocktail girl." She looked up at the bartender. "I'll have a rosé, please."

"Have you eaten?"

"I grabbed some quick room service before coming down." Actually, Nixon had called for the food. Maybe because he'd wanted to make sure she ate before coming down here? She wasn't sure if that was because eating with Rad would make it a date, or maybe he hadn't wanted her to drink on an empty stomach.

One side of Rad's mouth lifted. "We could always get dessert after."

"Maybe." Probably not. She cleared her throat. "Why don't you tell me about your content ideas?"

His fingers tapped against the bar, eyes never leaving hers. "I have many. This fair has been in the works for a while, and I want it to be a great success. When I approached Beth about the idea, she was quick to get involved."

That was unexpected. "It was your idea?"

"It was. I want it to become a fun family event for people all over—not just this country but the world."

The man dreamed big. "Do you have a background in this kind of stuff?"

He sipped what looked like whiskey. "I have a business degree. And with Beth's background in event management, I knew we'd be a great team. Not to mention the family ties. The woman's more like a sister than a cousin."

"That's really nice."

Her rosé was set in front of her, and she took a sip, letting the cool bubbles tingle over her tongue.

"When Beth showed me your social media channels and the engagement you got, I knew we needed you on the team. Have you always wanted to be an influencer?"

Her eyes twitched to look behind her at Nixon. She wasn't sure why. Hell, she didn't understand the pull toward him at all. "I like to think of myself as an event marketer. I studied marketing in college. It was while I was at school that I started my social media accounts, and they just kind of took off."

"And you enjoy it?"

"I love it. I'm my own boss. I can take or leave jobs, so my time is my own. More than that, though, my business is my baby. Something I've built from the ground up."

He nodded, staring at her mouth for a second before lifting his eyes again. "Well, I'm very glad you took this job."

"Me too. So, the content ideas?"

He frowned and nodded. "Right, the content ideas."

CHAPTER 8

$\mathcal{N}$ixon's fingers tightened around his glass of beer. The fucking guy was touching her *again*. Light grazes on the arm or shoulder when she spoke. She pulled away every time, but he always touched her in some seemingly innocent way again.

She'd removed her jacket, so the asshole was touching bare skin. He'd been doing that kind of shit all goddamn night, and every time he did, it took every scrap of self-restraint Nixon possessed to remain where he was. To not cross the space between them and rip his hand off.

He ground his teeth as he kept an eye on everyone in the bar. He was a professional, but right now, he was distracted. He'd never had to work so damn hard to focus on his job.

When his phone vibrated in his pocket, he pulled it out to see it was Nate.

Nate: Hey. I'm leaving for a mission tomorrow so will be offline for a few days. Just wanted to check that everything's okay before I become unreachable.

Okay? Nothing felt like it was in the vicinity of okay.

Nixon: The asshole left a comment on her latest post, but other than that, there's been nothing.

Nate: What did it say?

Nixon: Shit about how he can't wait to meet her.

Nate: Fuck, that makes me angry! I'm glad you're there to watch her back.

He looked up to see Rad leaning too far into her space.

Nixon's muscles vibrated, and he had to remind himself that punching the guy would lead to assault charges.

Nixon: She's safe with me.

It was a half-truth. She was safe from *others*. Like this asshole, Rad. But Nixon wasn't so sure she was safe from him. Because right now, he was a step away from throwing her over his shoulder and carrying her back to her room.

He was just lowering his phone when a tall blonde woman approached his table. "Hey. Couldn't help but notice that you're all alone over here."

"I prefer to drink alone."

The woman didn't seem deterred by his words. She leaned forward, her low-cut top revealing a hell of a lot of cleavage. "Maybe that's because you haven't had the right company before."

"I'm not interested in company."

Either his words didn't compute or she didn't care, because instead of walking away, she slipped around the table to touch his shoulder. "You seem tense. Maybe I can buy you a drink and—"

He stopped listening to the woman when he saw Rad's hand touch Finley's back…again.

Finley visibly tensed, her spine straightening as her hand went to his shoulder to push him away.

But the asshole didn't budge.

Nixon's restraint snapped and he was across the room in a second. There was a faint protest from the woman behind him, but he ignored it.

The second he reached the bar, he grabbed Rad's arm and pulled it away.

Rad stood, face red. "Hey, what are you—"

"When a woman pushes you away, you fucking shift back, asshole." He got so close that he could see every line on the guy's face.

Rad's eyes widened. "I didn't—"

"You *did*. If I catch you doing it again, I'll put you on the floor. Understand?"

The man's chest rose and fell, the red stain in his cheeks darkening.

"I said, do you understand?" Nixon's voice was louder now, even as he lowered his head a fraction.

Soft fingers touched his elbow. "Nixon—"

"I understand," Rad said, his tone clipped.

"Good." He turned and grabbed Finley's clutch and jacket from the bar, then slipped his fingers around her wrist. "We're leaving."

He started moving, the click of her heels trailing beside him.

He almost expected Rad to stop them. Tug her arm. Maybe step in front of them. Nixon almost *wanted* him to because then he'd have a reason to follow through on his threat and put a fist in his face.

But the asshole remained where he was. Maybe he was smarter than Nixon thought.

When he reached the elevator, he stabbed the button. It opened and he pulled her inside.

He felt her gaze on him the entire way up, like she was trying to assess his mood. It was dark, and that darkness just made him fucking angry. He shouldn't be so attached to her. He shouldn't be letting the asshole who'd touched her affect him so much.

It was only once they were in his room that he finally released her wrist and opened the connecting door. "Go."

When she didn't, his voice rose. "Finley, *go*."

She didn't. She stepped closer. "Are you okay?"

No, he wasn't. And he hated that. He hated this connection he felt to her.

He dropped the clutch and jacket onto the desk, then moved over to the bar and poured himself a shot of whiskey. He needed hard liquor and he needed it now. He needed the burn. The fire in his gut.

"Nixon—"

"He was all over you, Finley. What would you have done if I wasn't there?"

"I would have moved away from him." Her head tilted. "Nixon, it was just a touch on the back."

"With an asshole like that, it's never *just* anything." He downed the whiskey. "For him, it's about sex. It's about intimacy. It's one step closer to getting you into bed."

"Like I said, I'd have stepped away from him. If you hadn't stepped in—"

"He would have ignored you. Maybe kissed you."

She shook her head. "No."

"Yes." He turned to look at her, mood dark. "If he had kissed you, I would have broken his jaw, and not a single part of me would have felt bad about that."

Her lips parted, a puff of air escaping with her gasp. "Why would you do that?"

"Because seeing the man touch you was already making me angry enough. Seeing him kiss you…that would have tipped me over the edge. And I've been on edge all. Damn. Night. Watching you with him. Watching you in that top." It was killing him. Every time she moved, the material of her shirt slid over her body like silk, leaving nothing to the imagination.

He wasn't sure if he expected anger from her. Maybe frustration. He got neither. Instead, she stepped forward, eliminating the space between them, and cupped his cheek. "I'm sorry tonight was hard for you."

His brows flickered. *She* was apologizing to *him*? After he'd just lost his shit at something that wasn't her fault?

The heat of her hand seeped into his cheek, thickening the air around them. When her gaze shifted to his mouth, something kicked in his chest.

In almost slow motion, she rose to her toes and kissed him.

* * *

FOR A MOMENT, Nixon's lips were still against hers. Then she nipped at his mouth, and suddenly, he gripped her hips. Almost without her permission, her body leaned into him, her lips swiping his a second time, and a quiet, whispered moan escaped her throat.

Her thumb moved across his cheek, letting the rough day-old beard scrape her smooth, cold skin.

When the hand on her hip slid to her back and pulled her flush against him, she gasped. The second her lips parted, he slipped his tongue inside, tasting her. Melding them together.

The kiss was fire. It was heat and intensity and passion.

She moaned deep in her throat, and the second the sound hit air, he turned, lifting and pressing her to the wall. He was everywhere. Against her chest. Her core.

When his hand slid below her top, settling on her bare waist, she wanted to melt. Turn into pure liquid for this man.

She grabbed at the strands of his hair, tugging and pulling. Trying to find herself an anchor, something, *anything* to hold on to.

Then his hand continued up the flesh of her side, her breath catching in her throat when he cupped her breast over her bra. She whimpered, a dull ache starting to throb through her lower belly. His tongue continued to stroke hers as he pushed the cup down and palmed her bare breast, his thumb finding her nipple and grazing it back and forth.

God, he narrowed her entire world to just him.

"Nixon…" She breathed his name between desperate kisses.

She was just lowering her hands to the hem of his shirt, was just touching the bare skin beneath it, when his mouth tore from hers.

Then she was on her feet, and he was two steps back, the expression on his face pure agony. Like he couldn't believe what he'd just done.

"I need you to leave," he rasped.

Her chest moved up and down so quickly that she wasn't able to get a single full breath. She stepped toward him. "Nixon—"

"Please, Finley. You need to leave before I do another stupid thing."

Stupid? He was calling their kiss, the way he'd held her, touched her, and set her on fire, *stupid*? While she'd been drowning in it…and not wanting to come up for air.

She swallowed, trying to keep the hurt from splintering over her face. Without a word, she grabbed her clutch and jacket, then turned and left, closing the connecting door after her. But she didn't walk away. Instead, she leaned her head back against the door and closed her eyes, willing her heart to return to normal. For the air flow to even out in her lungs.

She'd kissed Nixon. And God, there weren't even words for what it had done to her. Completely torn her apart.

Her lips tingled, and she grazed her fingers over them, still feeling him there, wishing she could tug him back.

For three more heartbeats, she leaned against the door, then she forced her legs to move forward, only stopping when she reached the bathroom. Lowering her clutch and jacket to the counter, she looked up at her reflection.

Jesus, she looked exactly like she felt…completely undone. Her lips were red, her eyes glazed, the tight peaks of her nipples pushing against the thin material of her shirt.

She looked like she'd been well and truly ravaged.

And the thing was, if he hadn't stopped, she wouldn't have either. Because no part of her had felt capable of pausing what they'd started.

Her phone dinged from inside her clutch, and her fingers trembled as she pulled it out.

Andi: How's everything going?

She nibbled her bottom lip, debating over whether to tell her best friend the truth. She was typing before she could stop herself.

Finley: I kissed him.

The text had barely been sent before her phone rang.

"Who?" Andi shrieked. "Don't tell me it was your bodyguard."

"It was Nixon."

"No!" She just about screamed the word. "You're joking!"

"I'm not. He was so angry about me having a drink with one of the fair organizers, and I cupped his cheek to make sure he was okay, and just…kissed him."

Her friend's gasp was loud over the line. "Oh my God, did he kiss you back?"

Oh, he'd definitely kissed her back. "Yep."

"God, it's like something right out of *The Notebook*. Was it good?"

Finley could have laughed. "It was the best kiss I've ever had. I felt like he was everywhere, like time temporarily stopped." She sucked in a deep breath. "Then he told me to leave before he did another stupid thing."

There was a pause. "*Another* stupid thing?" Some of the excitement left Andi's voice.

"Yeah."

"Did it feel stupid to *you*?"

"No." She ran her finger over the edge of the counter. "It felt so right that if he hadn't stopped, I'd still be in his room."

In his arms…his mouth on hers. A shudder rocked her spine.

"So you need to work out what his deal is."

Finley almost laughed. "I don't know if it's that easy."

"Men are like presents with multiple layers of wrapping. You've got to peel back each layer of paper to see what's underneath."

She was shaking her head before Andi finished speaking. "I didn't come here for a relationship, Andi. I came here to work."

"We rarely go looking for love. It just finds us."

Love…ha. That was not what was happening here. Lust? Sure.

She toed off her shoes. "I'm wrecked. I might jump in the shower and go to bed."

"Tell me you're going to keep me posted."

Would there be more things to keep her friend posted *on*? The thought of never kissing the man again made her belly do a sad turn. "When do I ever not tell you something?"

"Good. Have a good night sleeping *right next door* to him, Fin."

Oh God. Did Andi need to remind her? It would probably be the most restless night's sleep of her life.

CHAPTER 9

Finley snuck a peek at Nixon beside her. The man had barely said two words to her all morning. In fact, he'd been quieter and a hell of a lot broodier than normal, something she hadn't thought possible.

She pursed her lips as they walked through the fairgrounds. On the Sunday before Christmas, it was busy.

She cleared her throat. "So, I thought we'd start with some ice-skating."

He nodded. Just…nodded. There was no "That sounds great, Fin." No little stories about how he'd skated in his youth. Not that she'd expected the latter, but any actual *words* would be nice.

"I think the last time I skated was about four years ago when I went to a rink with Andi," Finley said, trying to draw some conversation from the man. "I wasn't great."

Another nod.

She sighed and moved faster, walking to the line to wait for ice skates. She told herself to keep her mouth shut. If he wanted to give her the cold shoulder after their kiss, that was up to him.

That lasted all of thirty seconds before she couldn't take the silence anymore and spun on him. "Are you gonna be like this the entire week?"

"Like what?"

Oh, he knew *like what*. "Moody, unsmiling, and barely saying two words a day to me?"

"I've said more than two words to you today."

Her eyes narrowed. "That's why I said *barely*."

"What would you like me to say?"

"I don't know, maybe 'Did you sleep well?' or 'The snow's beautiful' or hell, you could even throw in an 'I'm looking forward to the fair today.'"

When the line moved, he stepped forward. "I assumed you slept well because you stepped out of your room smiling. I prefer the sun to snow. And I don't look forward to this fair."

Well, if there was ever a man who personified the Grinch, it was this one.

She stopped at the skates booth, surprised when Nixon gave his size. She'd been sure he wouldn't join her on the ice, maybe using the excuse that wearing skates would make it too hard to chase down a bad guy.

When their skates were on, she stepped onto the ice first, grabbing the railing around the perimeter so tightly that her knuckles turned white. She and ice did not mix well. But this wasn't about being great, and she wanted to portray that to her followers. The fun part was giving things a go.

She was just letting go of the railing, moving across the ice *very* slowly, when Nixon came gliding up beside her.

What the hell? The man skated like he'd been training his entire life! Were men like him just so physically gifted that they could do *everything*?

"How are you so good at this?"

"I had a client who was a professional skater. I made sure I learned the basics in case I needed to get to her quickly."

She paused. Wow, that was dedication. "Why did she need a bodyguard?"

"Similar situation to yours. Some asshole fan was targeting her."

"Was she okay?"

"Yeah. I got the guy about two months into the protective detail, when he was hiding in the bushes outside her townhouse."

A shudder rocked her body. "How do these people find our addresses?"

Nixon met her gaze. "When people put their lives online, they give away more than they think. There are usually stores in the background of photos. Street names. Even just posting the food you eat when you go out can give you away. Then, once these assholes know where you are, they start seeing patterns in your routine. Like maybe you go to Pilates on Wednesdays and the grocery store on Fridays."

Her skin chilled, a sick feeling churning in her belly. She posted a lot of her life online. But that was her job. Her follower count and interaction was what booked her events and paid her mortgage.

"That's sick," she said quietly.

"Obsession is a great motivator."

Obsession… She had become someone's *obsession*. Involuntarily, her breathing quickened, and her feet became unsteady.

"Hey."

She turned her head toward Nixon too quickly, and her skate slipped. She yelped as air rushed over her skin. Scrunching her eyes, she expected her butt to hit the ice, but strong arms wrapped around her, catching her before she could fall. Then his warmth surrounded her.

She opened her eyes to find Nixon right in front of her, his big chest taking up her field of vision until she raised her gaze. Her lips parted at the sight of his mouth so close, eyes so intense.

"Are you okay?" he asked in a gruff voice.

She nodded, struggling to make words work. "Thank you. You reacted so quickly." She'd barely recognized what was happening before he'd spun and grabbed her.

"Like I said, I've had a bit of practice."

Finley wrapped her fingers around his upper arms, feeling his biceps contract. "I'll, um, just get some footage and we can get off the ice."

For a moment, he was quiet, and for once she didn't mind. Because it was accompanied by his dark eyes on her. His gentle touch. Then he skated back a fraction, his hands on her hips. "Are you steady?"

Not even a little bit. "Yes."

He nodded and released her, then returned to her side.

She forced the small tremble from her fingers as she took some footage with her phone. She filmed the rink around her, carefully avoiding any glimpse of Nixon, continuing to skate as she went. Twice more, she almost fell. Both times, he was there to grab her. Wrap his fingers around her arm and steady her. Every time he touched her, she had to remind herself to breathe. To keep the absolute flurry of emotions inside her from showing on her face.

When she was finally done, she breathed a sigh of relief that she was off the ice. She was not what one would call a physically gifted person. And any new skills took time to learn. Certainly a lot longer than the hour she'd been in skates.

After finding a seat, they both put their shoes back on. Then she took a few minutes to review the footage while Nixon watched the rink. The man was always watching the people around them. She couldn't deny it made her feel safe.

Halfway through the video, something on the screen caught her attention.

She frowned, pausing the footage and zooming in on the trees in the background. A gasp slipped from her chest, and she shot to her feet. "Oh my God!"

Nixon was up and beside her in a moment. "What?"

Her gaze lifted from the phone to the exact spot in the woods. "Someone was behind the trees up there. And it looked like he was watching us."

The words had barely left her mouth when there was movement in the woods.

A man stepped out from behind a tree, clear as day. He was too far away for her to see the features of his face, but he was wearing the same red jacket as in the video.

Nixon cursed and pushed her toward the ground. "Stay down."

* * *

NIXON WAS RUNNING before he could stop himself. He jumped the perimeter fence and sprinted toward the tree the asshole hid behind, the air whipping across his face as his feet sank into the snow.

When he saw the back of the guy weaving through the trees, Nixon forced his body to move faster. He couldn't let this asshole escape.

Anger pummeled through his chest as he leapt over a tree stump. The guy had been staring right at her, and Nixon hadn't noticed. He'd been so fixated on Finley and making sure she didn't fall that he'd missed the threat.

When traffic sounded from a street in the distance, he swore under his breath and sped up again. It took too much time to reach the road, and once he did, he stopped, gaze searching for the asshole.

But he was gone.

Fuck.

He wanted to turn and punch his fist into a tree. To make the weight of his frustration over letting the man slip through his fingers drown in pain. The asshole had been right fucking *there*, yet he'd slipped away.

With gritted teeth, Nixon turned and jogged back to Finley, a new anxiety coiling in his chest that he'd left her alone for so long.

When he reached the fence, he climbed over, gaze going straight to Finley where she stood by the rink, arms wrapped around her waist.

The air rushed from his chest. The second he was near enough, he gripped her shoulders. "Are you okay?"

She nodded quickly, fear and worry glazing her eyes. "Are you?"

A muscle in his cheek clicked. He was far from fucking okay. "I lost him."

"But you're not hurt?"

"I'm not hurt."

Relief washed over her face. "That's good."

"Are you done?"

She nodded quickly. "We can go."

Nixon would be relieved if it wasn't for the fact they'd be back tomorrow. A vein in his temple throbbed as he shot one more look toward the woods before slipping an arm around her waist and turning toward the parking lot.

As they drove back to the resort, he tried to keep his damn mouth shut, but he couldn't. "You need to leave."

She frowned at him, her arms still crossed tightly at her belly. "What?"

"Being here is too dangerous, Finley. He knows exactly where you are, and you're too exposed at the fair."

"Nixon, I told you, I committed to this job, and I need to see it through. And I do not want to go to some unknown location and hide."

His fingers tightened on the wheel. "So stay in the resort until we've locked him down."

"When will that be, Nixon? How will we draw him out if I'm not out there? We don't know who he is, what he looks like. I can't just hide for an indefinite period of time. This is my job. My *life*."

"If that asshole wanted to shoot you from the trees, then he could have. Fuck, there were dozens of other people who could have been caught in the crossfire."

She flinched, and he instantly hated himself for that comment. For insinuating that, by not leaving, it would be her fault if an innocent bystander got shot.

"We don't even know if the guy in the woods was him. And even if it was, he's never directly hurt me or threatened to hurt me. I'm not running away and hiding. I will finish the job I accepted." Her voice was flat.

"Finley—"

"What would the end game be if I just hid in the resort and we *didn't* find him, Nixon? Would I go to some random location and hide out for an indefinite period of time? Letting followers forget about me and allowing my business to crumble?"

Jesus Christ, this woman. She was too damn stubborn. "It would give us time to find him."

"But you might not."

When they reached the resort, she was out of the car before he'd even pulled to a stop. He cursed, rushing to catch up. He set a hand on the small of her back as he guided her inside.

At their rooms, he entered through his first, checking that space, then hers, before giving her the all clear.

She went straight into her room and closed the connecting door with a resounding thud.

Nixon ran frustrated fingers through his hair.

Fuck, he was an asshole. But he was an asshole who cared about her safety. He understood what she was saying, and yes, hiding would make the job of finding this guy take longer. But in his eyes, that was worth it. Her safety was worth whatever time it cost.

With a growl, he turned back toward the connecting door and pulled it open—

He stopped at the sight of Finley, sitting on the bed, tears in her eyes and her sleeve pulled up…to reveal a cut on her arm.

CHAPTER 10

Finley gasped when Nixon threw open the door. He looked big and angry and dangerous.

Shit.

Quickly, she tugged her sleeve down and scrubbed the tears from her eyes even though she knew it was too late. He'd seen everything.

She tried to rise, but Nixon was across the room before she could move, lowering to his haunches in front of her and wrapping his fingers around her arm. Gently, he pushed up the sleeve of her shirt, growling low in his throat when he revealed the gash. "How did this happen?"

"It's nothing."

His gaze shifted from the cut to her face, his brows slashed together. "It's not *nothing*. You're hurt. Tell me how this happened."

She swallowed, hesitating a beat too long.

His eyes widened. "Did *I* do this? When I pushed you down?"

"It was my fault," she said quickly. "I left my skates on the ground behind me, and I fell on one."

His eyes darkened, an emotion she couldn't identify slipping over his face.

"I'll be back." His words were short and clipped.

He moved back into his room and returned a second later with a small bag. He sat beside her on the bed and opened it, revealing a first aid kit. He slipped his finger around her wrist again, his touch tender and light.

Carefully, he used an antiseptic to clean the cut. "Why didn't you tell me you got hurt?"

She lifted a shoulder. "It didn't hurt that much. And I was distracted by what had just happened."

"But it hurts enough for you to be upset now."

God, she hated that he'd seen her in tears. "I'm not crying because of the cut."

His gaze flashed up. "Then why are you upset?"

"I cry when I'm frustrated. I don't know why, it's just something I've always done. Sometimes I cry when I'm angry too."

And God, she was both of those things right now.

Another tear fell down her cheek, but before she could scrub it away, he reached up and grazed it away with the pad of his thumb. His touch was so gentle that she wanted to lean into it. Let his calm seep into her bones.

"I'm sorry you're frustrated," he said softly.

"I know you don't understand me staying," she said with a sigh. "But I've got no one to rely on but myself. The Hunters are family, but they're not blood related, and I would never want to rely on them financially. Nate has already done too much by hiring you. I'm proud of the business I've built, and I put everything into making it a success."

"I understand the need to make something of yourself," he said quietly.

He held her gaze for one more intense beat before grabbing a bandage from his first aid kid and wrapping it around her forearm. The cut wasn't huge, but it was too big for a Band-Aid.

"Your sleeve was pulled up when you fell?"

She nodded. If it hadn't been, it might have saved her from the wound.

His jaw clenched, and she could see the emotions swirling in his dark eyes. The blame he was putting on himself.

Unable to stop herself, she reached out and cupped his cheek. "Hey. It's *not* your fault. You wanted me down in case the guy had a weapon. You chased after him. You did everything you could to keep me safe."

"I hurt you."

"*No.* You didn't put the skate there. I did. I fell onto it. It was an accident. You would never intentionally hurt me." She might not have known this man for long, but she knew that.

His gaze shifted between her eyes. "You're right, I wouldn't."

Her heart thumped.

When the bandage was on, he swiped his thumb across her forearm. "Have you eaten?"

She shook her head, any words getting lodged in her throat. Stuck.

"Let's go get dinner."

He wanted to have dinner with her? As in, something other than room service? Where had her broody protector gone? "Where are we going to go?"

"I heard the restaurant downstairs is pretty good."

She tilted her head. "You want to eat at a fancy resort restaurant with me?"

"Yes." The word came so quickly, and with so much certainty, that her breath caught.

"Because I'm upset?"

"Because we both need to eat, and I want to do that with you. Plus, I'm getting sick of eating in here."

She laughed, not believing him for a second. The room and room service were amazing.

"Okay. But I must warn you, I'll probably order eggnog."

He made a face of disgust. "Why would you do that?"

"Because it's less than a week before Christmas, and it's the only time of year they serve it."

"Maybe this place doesn't—"

"They do. I already checked."

He shook his head, obviously trying to look unhappy about it, but she saw the ghost of a smile on his face. "You're something else, Finley."

Before she could ask if that something else was good or bad, he headed into his room. "I'm just gonna change."

The second he was gone, she pulled off her sweatshirt and rummaged through her clothes for something pretty. She tugged out a pale blue knit shirt with a high neck and some tight jeans. Perfect.

Once she was dressed, she threw on a bit of makeup, then looked at her reflection. Her eyes were still a bit red rimmed, but they were also wide and bright.

She'd just slipped her feet into heels when the knock came.

A small shiver ran down her spine at the sight of Nixon. He only wore jeans and a dark sweater, but the guy could wear a potato sack and still be the most handsome man she'd ever seen.

When they stepped into the hall, he placed a familiar hand on the small of her back, his fingers spread wide. Immediately, her skin turned hot and her belly did a little flip. She liked having this man touch her. And that kind of scared her. Because their days together were numbered.

* * *

Nixon tried not to cringe as Finley sipped her eggnog. Even if he *were* a fan of Christmas, he still wouldn't drink the stuff. It was raw egg and milk. The only part of the drink that sounded appetizing was the bourbon.

"How is it?" he asked as she lowered the glass to the table.

"Amazing. Tastes like home. The Hunter home, that is. My mother didn't care to do anything for the holidays, so Andi always invited me to her place."

"Why didn't she celebrate the holidays?"

"Because she didn't care. Even before my father died, my mother was a serial dater. She cared more about her latest boyfriends than she ever did about me. Not that any of those boyfriends lasted. She was very good at getting a man but terrible at keeping him."

"Why did they never stay?"

"Because it never took long for her less desirable traits to come out. She was possessive. Jealous. She'd start talking about a ring after a month. I think her longest relationship was…" Finley wrinkled her nose in thought. "Six months, maybe? And man, I felt sorry for him. He really liked her, but she made his life hell until he finally couldn't take it anymore."

"I'm sorry."

She shrugged. "A lot of kids had it worse than me. And I was lucky because I had Andi. Her family started filling the gaps. Birthdays. Christmases. And when I got Andi, I got Nate too. They were close in age, so he became like a brother."

"Not Erik, though?" Nixon knew about Nate's older brother, who'd been a Marine, although his friend didn't talk about Erik very often.

The corners of Finley's mouth turned down. "Erik's a bit older than me, so I never got to know him that well. Then eight years ago, he lost…a lot. He's been really hard to reach since then. But he just moved back to Redwood and is reconnecting with his family. From what Andi's told me, his new neighbor is having quite the effect on him."

He chuckled. "A good woman can do that to a man."

Her smile softened. "You should do that more often."

"What?"

"Laugh. It looks good on you."

He sipped his beer. At this point, he'd probably plaster a smile on his face all goddamn day if the woman asked him to. Especially after what he'd done this afternoon.

Fuck, he still wanted to kick his own ass for shoving her to the ground so hastily. It was his fault she'd been hurt. His fault she'd been in her room, upset, with a huge gash on her arm. And he was pretty sure if he hadn't walked in when he had, she'd never have told him about it.

What did that say about him? About the way he'd been making her feel?

"So, what about you?" she asked, taking another sip of eggnog. "Is your family as tragic as mine?"

He knew she'd been going for a joke, but he couldn't stop the violent twist of his gut at the question. "I don't celebrate the holidays with my parents either."

She frowned. "How come?"

"When my older sister was eighteen, she was killed," he said bluntly. "As a family, you don't come back from that."

The color drained from Finley's face. "Oh my God. I'm so sorry."

He wasn't sure why he'd told her. He'd never told *anyone* except his SEAL brothers and Jacob.

Bile churned in his gut at the memory. "It was a long time ago." But as he'd learned, time didn't heal all wounds. It allowed you a few moments of reprieve every so often, when you could almost forget. But the pain always returned.

"How old were you?" she asked quietly.

"Sixteen. Our parents were out, and I was in my room when it happened."

If possible, her face went even whiter. Shit, he needed to stop talking. But for some reason, Finley made him want to share everything. To expose all the broken bits that were his life.

"Nixon…that would have been…" She didn't finish. Maybe because there were no fucking words for what it was. Torture.

Hell. A nightmare he could never wake up from. "Did they find her…killer?"

He cleared his throat. "Yeah. The guy was her high school boyfriend. He couldn't handle it when she broke up with him. He began to stalk her. No one took it as seriously as they should have. When he entered the house, I had my headphones on and had no idea what was happening until it was too late."

Visible tears gathered in Finley's eyes. She reached over and laid a hand on top of his. "I'm so sorry. About everything. That your childhood was taken away too early. That you lost someone you loved. And that your family fell apart because of it."

Usually, sympathy made his skin crawl. And when that sympathy was accompanied by any form of touch, he ran from it. Because it burned him. Cut at his flesh. But right now, Finley's hand on his felt like the only thing keeping the demons inside him at bay. The only thing keeping him here and whole.

When her hand began to pull away, he turned his over and slipped his fingers around hers. Her eyes widened just a fraction, but she didn't say anything. And that silence, the way her fingers wrapped around his hand to hold him back…it was comfortable.

It was only the waitress setting their meals in front of them that had him releasing her and her moving back. But, fuck, that loss felt heavy. And all he wanted to do was pull her back in again.

$\mathcal{N}$ixon remained close to Finley as they walked through the fair. It was evening. They'd arrived later today specifically so she could get some night footage. He'd thought there might be fewer people. There weren't. If possible, it seemed busier. More people, less light…fuck, that put him on edge.

He inched closer to her.

They'd spent most of the evening so far eating hot dogs and exploring the Christmas lights, Finley recording and snapping photos as they went.

He'd begun following her channels closely. Her TikTok account in particular got a lot of traffic. So many goddamn eyes knowing exactly where she was. Exactly what she was doing. The bodyguard in him hated that.

"Thank you," she said softly, hip nudging his.

He looked down at her soft smile. Things felt different today. *She* felt different. Softer. Like she didn't need to fight him on every little thing. But maybe that was partly because he'd stopped fighting her too.

"For what?"

"For not being a total pain in my ass about coming here this evening."

Oh, he'd wanted to be. "I've learned that it's a losing battle. You know where I stand on the matter."

"Well, all the same, I appreciate it." She lifted a shoulder. "Plus, it's kind of nice having someone come on a trip with me, even if you were an unwelcome guest at first."

His lips twitched. "You saying you like having me here now?"

"Today, yes. Traveling from place to place can get a bit lonely. Some people take partners or friends, but I don't have a partner, and my best friend is too busy saving lives."

Something inside him twisted at the thought of this beautiful woman being lonely. It was so fucking strong that he almost wanted to stop them and cup her cheek. Tug her into his arms.

He just stopped himself. Because what would he say? That she had *him*, so it was all okay now? She didn't. Not really. Nate had only hired him for this trip. After this, if they hadn't caught the guy, he was hoping like hell she agreed to the safe house.

Another fucking twist of his gut.

He cleared his throat. "I'm glad I haven't completely ruined the trip for you."

She laughed. "There's still time."

They were just about to step onto the bridge when a voice sounded behind them.

"Finley."

Nixon's muscles tensed, his jaw ticking at the sound of that asshole's voice. He turned to see Rad striding toward them. His gaze moved over Nixon for a moment, eyes narrowing before shifting to Finley. "I just wanted to check in on how everything's going."

Finley smiled, but the smile was tight and didn't quite reach her eyes. "It's been really good. Today I filmed the food and how this place looks in the evening. It's all beautiful. My viewers will love it."

"Great." He cocked his head. "Have you had a horse and sleigh ride?"

A vein throbbed in Nixon's temple.

Finley's brows rose. "Not yet."

It took too much goddamn strength to not ball his hands into fists. Because he knew what was coming next.

"Would you like to join me?"

Yep. Nixon was gonna hit the guy.

"I'll have you back to your assistant safe and sound," Rad said, stepping forward. "I promise."

The prick.

Nixon wasn't sure if he stepped forward or maybe just tilted toward Rad, but Finley reached out and touched his now-fisted hand, the warmth of her fingers slipping into his skin, providing a scrap of calm.

"I actually promised Nixon a sleigh ride before we go tonight. Sorry. Then we have to be getting back to our hotel so I can edit some of my footage. But maybe I'll catch you tomorrow."

Nixon could just about see the effort it took for Rad's face to remain as it was. He gave a sharp nod as Finley grasped Nixon's wrist and tugged him toward the sleigh rides.

The tightness in his chest eased, but that wasn't just because of Finley's words. It was the warmth of her skin against his. The way she stepped close enough to graze his side.

She stopped beside the sleigh, and the guy holding the reins smiled at them. "Ride?"

Finley nodded. "Yes, please."

When she tried to climb up, Nixon set his hands on her waist and lifted her. She gasped but quickly shuffled to the side. He climbed up and sat beside her. The seating area was small, and with the limited space, his entire side touched hers.

The driver snapped the reins and they started moving.

Nixon had to remind himself to relax. The ride felt romantic. Intimate.

Finley beamed up at him. "Okay, you cannot tell me this isn't getting you just a bit excited for Christmas."

Those words slammed him back to reality. "No."

Her smile turned into a frown, but she recovered quickly. "Fine. But you're not having a terrible time, right?"

"Depends on what your definition of terrible is."

This time she laughed, and that sound shot straight to his gut. "Definitely not a night of hot dogs and sleigh rides in the snow, but then, you are the Grinch of Christmas, so maybe in your eyes?"

"The Grinch?"

Finley's jaw dropped. "You don't know who the Grinch is?"

"Nope."

Her gasp was loud. "Nixon...no!"

His mouth twitched. The woman looked at him with such devastation that he had to put her out of her misery. "I'm joking. I'm pretty sure everyone in this country has been exposed to that movie."

She laughed and shook her head. "Thank God. For a second there, I thought you were literally living on another planet." Then she seemed to take a moment to consider her next words. "Have you seen *How the Grinch Stole Christmas*?"

"Do you think I've seen *How the Grinch Stole Christmas*?"

Her brown eyes studied him, then widened. "You haven't."

She was right. He'd never sat through it as a kid, and as an adult, he wouldn't go near it with a ten-foot pole.

"Okay, we need a movie night, and we need it fast," she said, seeming far too excited by the idea.

His heart warred with his head. Because the idea of sitting beside this woman throughout an entire movie felt good. And a part of him wanted that...while the other part ran from it.

He cleared his throat. "I don't think so."

"Hmph. Fine, but let it be known, when you're on your death

bed and you missed out on watching one of the greatest movies ever created, I tried."

"Not gonna happen."

When the sleigh went over a hump, Finley gasped and grabbed his arm. It reminded him of the way she'd grabbed him on the plane. Only then, she'd just been a pretty stranger. Now, every touch felt familiar.

"You okay?" he asked, voice too gruff.

"Yeah." But she didn't remove the hand from his arm. Instead, she looked up at him, and that stare chained him to the moment.

He should pull his arm away, or at least look away from her. He should fucking run from Finley and what she did to him. But no part of him felt capable of that. Everything she was called to his soul. Like a melody made just for him.

As if his hand had a mind of its own, his fingers slipped through hers.

Her eyes softened, her bottom lip disappearing between her teeth. With his other hand, he reached up and tugged the lip out with the pad of his thumb. But then he didn't move his hand. Instead, he grazed her bottom lip, slowly, back and forth.

Her lips parted, her gaze lowering to his mouth.

Fuck, she destroyed him.

His head screamed at him to take his hand away. To look away. But his fucking body betrayed him as he lowered his head and kissed her.

Immediately, the press of her mouth against his made his heart thump in his chest. Something inside him changed. Relaxed. Made sense for the first time in his goddamn life.

When her lips separated, he slipped his tongue inside, tasting her. Letting her sweetness sift through him.

The kiss was silent, but it was also loud, deafening the world around him. Turning everything and everyone to nothing.

Her fingers swept up his chest, and he felt it as if she was touching his bare skin. Like she'd burned through the material of his clothes.

He threaded his fingers into her hair. He wanted to deepen the kiss. To lay this woman down and bathe in her. It was only when the sound of talking penetrated the fog that he came back from reality.

They were on a sleigh. In public. Fuck, he wasn't even watching their surroundings.

He lifted his head, and Finley's groan almost undid him. Almost had him slipping back to her again.

"I need to stop doing that," he said, fingers still tangled in her hair.

"Why?"

"Because you're my client."

She shook her head. "No. I didn't hire you."

That wasn't how it worked. "You still are."

"Nixon, I—" She stopped, frowning at something over his shoulder.

He twisted in the direction she'd looked, hand going to his concealed Glock. "What is it?" When he saw nothing, he turned back to her.

She shook her head. "Nothing."

"Finley—"

"It was nothing. I'm just being paranoid."

Before he could push, the sleigh stopped, the driver's voice booming. "Okay! End of the line."

* * *

FINLEY'S EYES SHOT OPEN. The hotel room was dark around her, the only light coming from the small digital clock beside the bed.

But something had woken her…

What?

She was a deep sleeper, so it had to be something loud. Had

someone made a noise from the hall? Maybe someone returning late to their room or ordering middle-of-the-night room service?

She leaned over to check her phone. Perhaps she'd forgotten to put it on silent and someone had texted?

Nope. The screen was black. It was switched off.

Could it have been nothing? It had taken her ages to fall asleep after that kiss on the sleigh ride with Nixon. Maybe she was just unsettled.

She dropped back onto the plush mattress. God, maybe with everything that was going on, she was just losing her damn—

A noise sounded from Nixon's room.

She shot up into a sitting position. It almost sounded like a growl.

Her pulse sped up, the deep thuds of her heart loud in her ears.

When it sounded again, this time louder, her breath caught. The sound was almost pained. Shuffling noises came next.

Her heart catapulted into her throat. Oh God, had someone broken into his room? Had someone attacked him, possibly while he was sleeping?

Moving on instinct, she climbed out of bed and walked silently to the connecting door. She was about to open it but stopped. If there was an intruder, she'd be an easy target. She needed a weapon.

She scanned the room, desperately looking for something. Anything. There was nothing. Absolutely—

Curtain rail. It wasn't optimal, but there was nothing else. It wasn't like the hotel kept knives in the rooms.

Quickly, she grabbed a chair and pushed it to the window. Once she was standing on the chair, she took the rod off the hooks, then slipped off the curtain. The rod was short but heavy and had a fancy point at the end. If she stabbed it at the attacker's ribs, it could do some serious damage.

Tightening her fingers around it, she rushed back to the door just as more rustling and growls sounded. Her heart gave one more hard thump—then she wrenched open the door, expecting to see movement and fighting. Expecting danger to surround her.

Instead, the room was dark and still.

When another growl came, her attention shot to the bed.

Nixon had kicked all the blankets down, and he was thrashing, his eyes closed. The look on his face…God, it was all pain.

Nixon…

For a moment, she stayed completely still, feet rooted to the spot, unsure whether to leave him and hope he came out of it or try to wake him.

When his head thrashed to the side again, a tortured groan tearing from his throat, she lowered the rod to the floor and climbed onto the bed.

She reached out to touch him, then pulled her arm back.

God, she had no idea what to do! There was every chance touching the man could make it worse.

"Nixon." She wasn't loud, but she wasn't quiet either.

He didn't stir. Not even a flicker of his eyelids.

She swallowed and lightly touched his shoulder. "Nixon."

Again, nothing.

The next sound he made was worse than the others. It sounded like it was torn from somewhere deep inside him.

Her heart cracked for the man.

Shit…she had to try something else. When he rolled to his side, facing her, she lay down beside him, shuffling so close she could see every line of pain on his face. Carefully, she placed a hand on his cheek and touched her forehead to his.

God, he was hot. And sweat beaded every inch of his skin.

She forced her breath to remain steady as she whispered, "You're safe, Nixon. You're okay."

At first, he kept growling and flinching, his chest moving so quickly that he couldn't be getting a single deep breath.

She repeated the same words, reminding Nixon that he was safe. That he was okay. And that he wasn't alone.

It took four more times for his movement to still. The noises to silence. Then, finally, his breathing evened out.

She didn't move right away. She kept her forehead against his and her palm to his cheek, scared that he'd fall back into whatever hell he'd found himself in if she shifted. But she couldn't stay here forever.

She was about to move when a word whispered from his lips. "Finley…"

Her heart clenched in her chest. Did he know she was here? She needed to get the heck out of here before he fully woke and found her in his bed.

Carefully, she lifted her hand from his cheek and rolled to her other side. She was mid-escape when a strong arm slipped around her waist and pulled her back into a hot, hard body.

Her muscles tensed, her body freezing. She didn't even take a breath.

Shit, shit, shit.

Slowly, she reached for his hand and tried to lift it. But the second she touched skin, the arm around her tightened, pulling her closer to the warm body behind her. The *almost naked* warm body, because Nixon was only wearing briefs.

Panic rattled in her chest.

What should she do? Stay? Wait for him to fall into a deeper sleep, then try again?

Yes. What other options did she have? She'd wait for him to go lax, then slip back to her room.

It would be fine.

She sighed and closed her eyes, letting his warmth, his hardness and strength, surround her. Calm her. Hold her.

CHAPTER 12

The sweet mix of lilacs and honey scented the air around Nixon, piercing his sleep, pulling him to the surface.

Finley. She was here, with him. Why? How?

He flexed his hand, feeling her soft skin beneath his fingertips. Then he felt the rest of her. The heat of her arm around his waist. The softness of her cheek against his chest.

His pulse sped up, confusion pricking at his skull. He should get up. End this connection between them and get the answers he needed. But if he did that, this moment would be shattered. She'd wake, and he wouldn't be holding her anymore. Her cheek wouldn't be pressed to his heart.

And no part of him wanted this moment to end.

Slowly, he opened his eyes to find her sprawled against him, her hair spread over his bare skin. Her chest rose and fell in slow succession while each exhale brushed his skin in long strokes of heat.

She wore the shortest pajama shorts he'd ever seen, half her ass on full display. And her top had risen up her ribs so that a hell of a lot of skin was not only showing but touching him.

Parts of his body hardened that had no business hardening. Not only that, but something flickered in his chest. It was hot and primal, and he had no fucking clue how to navigate it.

What the hell was going on? They were in his room. The connecting door was open. So she'd come to him. Why? And why couldn't he fucking remember her getting into bed with him? Hell, why hadn't he woken when she had? He was a light sleeper. He usually woke at the slightest sound.

He knew the exact moment she woke. Her breathing changed rhythm from long, deep draws to shallow inhalations. Her hand moved across his bare stomach and chest in almost a caress, causing his dick to twitch, which he could only hope like hell she didn't notice.

He expected her to push up. Say something. Instead, she remained completely still, maybe scared to move in case he was asleep and she woke him.

"Finley."

Her chest stopped moving. But still, she remained silent.

"I know you're awake."

She cringed, then slowly pushed up on his chest to look at him. And fuck, her eyes destroyed him. Not only that, but he saw too much cleavage. And the way her hard nipples pushed against the thin material of her top was like an assault on his senses.

She swallowed. "Hey."

"What are you doing in here?"

She nibbled her bottom lip. Immediately, his focus shifted down, his body locking as the need to reach out and tug that lip out like he had the previous night hit him hard.

"You were having a nightmare."

Her words made the heat inside him turn cold and dread pit his gut.

Fuck. He'd had one of his nightmares and she'd heard? Not only that, she'd *seen* it.

"I was worried," she continued, her gaze roaming his face. "I thought maybe…there was someone in here and you were in trouble."

His brows slashed together. "You thought someone was in here, and you decided to come in instead of running in the other direction? God, Finley, did you even have a weapon?"

"Yes." Her head turned, and he followed her gaze to a curtain rod.

Shit. "Finley. If you ever think I'm in trouble again, you run *away*, not toward me."

"No. I'm not running if you need help."

"What if someone was in here with a gun?"

"Then I'd have distracted him long enough to give you a chance to get the upper hand."

God, this woman…

He shook his head in wonder. Then her thumb grazed his flesh, and he was again reminded of just how little clothing they were both wearing.

"I'm sorry I woke you," he said in a voice that was too gruff. "This time of year tends to make the nightmares worse."

Why the hell had he gone and added that last part?

Her eyes softened. "You don't need to apologize."

"Why did you stay in here?"

"I wasn't going to." Her cheeks shaded a pretty pink. "You weren't waking, so I lay beside you and whispered that you were safe. When you finally calmed, I started to crawl away, but you wrapped your arm around my waist and pulled me against you."

So even when he was unconscious, he was irrevocably drawn to this woman. "So you stayed."

"So I stayed." Her thumb swiped over his chest again. Once more, his heart thumped. "I meant to leave when you relaxed, but I guess I fell asleep."

No wonder he felt so damn well rested. "Thank you for waking me. And being willing to curtain rod an intruder."

Her lips turned up. "Hey…I would have taken that intruder down."

Another fucking twitch of his cock. "I believe you."

At the beat of silence, the smile slowly slipped from her lips, her attention shifting down to his mouth. Almost of its own accord, his hand lifted to her cheek, then behind her head, before tugging her down until their mouths met.

Finley softened into him, her moan a quiet whisper in the room. When her fingers slid over his chest, his heart began to race. He ran his tongue over the seam of her lips. She opened for him, and he slipped his tongue into her mouth, dueling with hers.

Immediately, he rolled them and pressed her to the mattress. Then his hand touched her bare stomach. Slowly, he slid up her ribs, her shirt rising with his hand, before settling over her breast. She moaned again, deeper, and that sound set off a storm in his chest.

He palmed her breast before finding her nipple with the pad of his thumb and grazing it lightly. Her breaths became choppy, her fingers digging into his shoulders, nails almost breaking skin.

God, this woman…her sounds, her softness…everything about her drove him fucking crazy.

He tore his mouth from hers and kissed down her cheek, then her neck. When he reached her chest, he took one pebbled nipple between his lips and sucked. The noise that rippled from her throat was something akin to torment. He wanted more. He wanted to fucking bathe in this woman's desire.

He ran his tongue over the tight bud, first in a circle, then flicking it back and forth.

Finley writhed beneath him, her fingers now pulling at the strands of his hair. When he switched to the other breast, it was the same thing.

He'd just trailed a line of kisses up her neck and was reaching for the waistband of her shorts when the hotel phone rang in her room.

For a moment, they both stilled.

He lifted his mouth and touched his forehead to hers. Their heavy breathing was a soft counterpoint to the jarring phone.

"I should get that," she breathed, disappointment coating her words.

He had to force himself to lean to the side. To uncage her from the bed. But even as she moved, his fingers twitched to tug her back to him.

Silently, she moved to her room. He got up and walked to the doorway, watching as she lifted the receiver.

"Hello?" There was a small pause. "Yes, this is Finley."

When her knuckles whitened, he closed the space between them.

"Okay. Thank you, I'll come get it." She hung up and turned, looking up at him. "A package has been left at reception for me."

* * *

"I'M COMING."

Nixon spun on her, moving so fast she almost fell back onto his bed. "You're not."

"Unless you plan on resorting to locking me in my room, which I would break out of by the way, I'm going down with you to get my package."

She'd never thrown clothes on so quickly in her life, because she knew—one second too long and the man would go down without her. Hell, he'd been dressed and had one hand on his door when she'd stepped into his room.

Anger blasted over his face. "We don't know what this package is. It could be dangerous."

She planted her fists on her hips. "I'm going."

"Finley." Her name was a growl.

She straightened her spine. "If you keep me here, I'll call them and tell them not to give you my package."

They shouldn't anyway, but knowing Nixon, he'd probably spew some words about them being together and being sent for her delivery.

He took two big steps forward, towering over her. She almost stepped back. Heck, she almost stumbled back. When the man wanted to intimidate someone, he could. But she refused to cower or step away.

"Finley—"

"I'm coming, Nixon."

His chest filled with a deep breath, then he cursed. "Fine. But I take the package, and I open it down there. We're not bringing it back to the room."

"Deal."

He shook his head, letting out a slew of curses before storming from the room. He was still muttering under his breath when they reached the elevator, and she was pretty sure she heard the words, *will be the death of me,* thrown in there.

"We don't even know that this package is from him," she said quietly, trying to diffuse the situation as the elevator moved.

"They said it was left at the front desk."

"Yeah, so it could have been left by a mail carrier. Andi and her entire family know we're here and it's four days until Christmas." But...the entire family had already given her their Christmas presents before she'd left, so she wasn't overly optimistic. Not that she'd be telling him that.

The doors opened and Nixon walked out. His steps were so long and fast, she took two strides for every one of his. She was basically running to keep up. As he walked, he pulled latex gloves onto his hands.

At reception, he said, "You have a package for Miss Dunkley."

"*I'm* Miss Dunkley," Finley said, pushing beside him.

The man nodded. "Yes, I think Joline left it down here." He turned and lifted a small package. The fine hairs stood on end at the sight of the red wrapping paper adorned with small

Christmas trees. There was also a big white bow. No postage, just a note that read *For Finley.*

"Who left this?" Nixon asked, his voice tightly controlled.

"I'm not sure, sir. Joline took the package, but she's currently helping another guest. I can ask for the information when she returns."

When Nixon didn't answer, just continued to grind his teeth like he was going to murder someone before spinning around, Finley smiled at the man. "That would be great. Thank you."

She followed Nixon to the couch in front of the fire. It wasn't until he was pulling at the ribbon that the nerves kicked in.

Like he heard her pulse pick up speed, he paused and studied her. "Last chance, Fin. I can do this on my own."

Even though her skin felt clammy and her belly sick, she shook her head. "No. I want to see what it is."

She had to. This was about her.

His jaw clenched, but he didn't say anything, just nodded.

Slowly, he opened the small cardboard box.

She gasped at what she saw.

Polaroid photos of the horse and sleigh ride the previous night.

Nixon lifted the photos out. They were crumpled, like someone had scrunched them up in anger.

One by one, he filtered through them. Pictures of her and Nixon looking into each other's eyes. Kissing.

Nausea rolled in her belly, but she forced it down. She'd fought to be here. She had to be strong enough to handle this.

There were six Polaroids in total. And below them, a note.

You let him touch you, but you're supposed to be mine. You shouldn't have done that. KJ.

Her skin chilled. The writing was a messy scrawl, like he'd been angry when he'd written it. He'd dug the pen so deeply into the paper, it had gone through in a couple places.

Nixon threw the note back into the box. For the first time, her gaze shifted up to see how furious he was. To witness the angry line of his mouth and eyes.

He looked ready to kill.

He lifted the box and stormed back to the desk. She rushed to follow. "We need to watch hotel security footage to see who left this."

The front desk attendant's brows rose. "Sir, that's not really done—"

"Now."

For a moment, the man looked uncomfortable, then he picked up the phone. "I just need to call my manager."

Ten minutes later, they were in a back office with multiple screens hung across the room. Once the security manager knew what he was looking for, he flicked through the footage.

Every second that ticked by had Finley growing more nervous. The door behind them opened, and a woman with a name badge that read Joline entered.

"Hi," she greeted nervously. "Paley told me you needed to know who left the package."

Finley smiled at her. "Yes. Was it a man or a woman? Or better yet, do you have a name?"

The questions had just left Finley's lips when the security man found the footage of the man stepping into the hotel foyer.

Finley gasped, and Nixon went so hard that every muscle in his body visibly bunched.

"It was a man. But I don't have a name, sorry," the woman said, her words competing with the buzzing in Finley's ears.

But they didn't need her to know his name. Because the man in the footage was Rad Hamilton.

"That footage goes to the police," Nixon said, stepping back and pulling his phone from his pocket. Then he moved from the room as he called the police. Again, Finley ran to keep up, listening to his side of the conversation as he explained the situation to the police.

When he hung up, he didn't move toward the elevators to go to their room. Instead, he beelined for the doors leading outside.

"Nixon, stop!"

He didn't. If anything, he moved faster. She ran outside after him and grabbed his arm just before he reached his car. "Nixon—"

"You need to go back to your room. I need to find this fucker and make sure he doesn't make a run for it before the police arrest him."

"You don't have your keys."

"I do." He pulled out of her hold and opened his car door.

Shit.

She ran around the vehicle, then pulled the passenger door open and slid inside.

Nixon flashed his angry eyes at her. "Get out, Fin. You're not coming."

"I am."

His chest rose, and he opened his mouth, presumably to yell at her, but she got in first.

"Unless you plan to drag me from the car and all the way upstairs—which I would yell and scream about, by the way—I'm coming."

Cementing her point, she pulled the seat belt across her body, then crossed her arms.

Nixon growled before grabbing the wheel tightly and pulling out of the lot.

"You realize this doesn't make sense, right?" she said quietly. "If Rad's behind the messages and gifts, do you really think he'd be dumb enough to leave the package in person?"

When Nixon didn't answer, she shook her head and leaned back in her seat. He'd barely put the car into park when he was out and storming toward the bridge. She hurried to keep up with him, but man, it was hard. He was fast and he wasn't even running.

They'd almost made it to the trailer door when it opened and Rad stepped out. His eyes widened when they landed on Nixon. Then he turned and tried to rush back inside, but Nixon grabbed him and shoved him into the side of the trailer.

"What the fuck is wrong with you?" Nixon yelled.

The color left Rad's face. "What are you talking about? Release me!"

"You take photos of me and Finley in the sleigh, then wrap them up in a box and leave them at our hotel?"

His mouth opened and closed. "I didn't—"

"You *did*." Nixon pulled him off the wall and shoved him back again. "The police are on their way to arrest your ass."

Finley gasped when the guy's head hit the trailer, hard. "Nixon—"

"Why?" Nixon growled, ignoring her.

Rad's voice grew a bit firmer, anger slivering into his words. "I *didn't* take photos of you and her."

"What's going on?" Finley turned to see Beth approaching the trailer, worry on her face. "Let him go!"

"No," Nixon said, voice a hard line. "He left a little package at our resort for Finley. Police will be here soon."

Beth frowned. "I asked him to take the package to the resort. Someone left it here at the trailer door, so I asked him to run it over to you. Why? What's going on?"

Nixon frowned, finally stepping back. Rad straightened his clothes, anger on his face.

Finley swallowed, gaze shifting from Rad to Beth. "I should have told you this earlier."

Beth cocked her head. "Told us what?"

"I have a stalker."

CHAPTER 13

"I'm not angry, Finley. I just wish you'd told me what was going on from the beginning," Beth said.

Finley swallowed, fingers tightening around the phone at her ear. She was back in her hotel room. She and Nixon had returned a few hours ago. The second news about the stalker had been revealed, Beth, Rad, and the police had worked with her and Nixon to file a report.

The police had taken the photos to see if they could get any prints, but Finley wasn't hopeful. This guy was no doubt smarter than that.

"I'm sorry," Finley said quietly, pulling at a loose thread on her yoga pants. "You've been so good to me, offering this job, and I didn't want to lose it or have you question whether I should be here. It was selfish."

"I wouldn't have taken the job away from you. I love your work. And your content from this fair has helped us make it the success it's been. I just would have put more security in place from the start."

God, the woman was too good to her. It was Christmas in four days, and somehow she'd managed to organize more security for the fair in an attempt to keep it safe not just for Finley but everyone who attended. "Thank you."

"No, thank *you*. People have come from all over the province of Ontario. You are worth your weight in gold, girl."

"I love that I've been able to help you and Rad." She sighed, relieved. "My visits will just be quick ones from here on out. I'll try some of your signature drinks from the pop-up café, maybe get footage of the kids playing in the snow. I also need to try tobogganing. Then that should be it."

They'd been due to fly out December thirtieth, but she was sure Nixon would be changing that to an earlier flight.

She should be happy at the prospect of leaving early, but she wasn't. They hadn't figured out what they were doing after this. No part of her wanted to go to a safe house with a random guard. And her time with Nixon was coming to an end.

Her heart gave a sad turn at the thought.

"It all sounds wonderful, Finley. You stay safe, okay? And let me know if I can help in any other way."

"I will. Thank you, Beth."

When the call ended, she glanced at the connecting door. Her legs twitched to go over there and talk to him. The only thing stopping her was the fact that the second they'd gotten back to the hotel, he'd immediately disappeared inside his room and hadn't come out.

If that didn't scream, *I want to be alone*, then nothing did. Whether he was annoyed about the package, the fact that she'd gone with him to the fair, or just a combination of everything, she wasn't sure.

But God, how had they been in bed kissing this morning, and now she didn't even feel like she could knock on his door?

With a sigh, she moved into the bathroom and turned on the shower. She was usually a morning-shower person, so showering at five in the evening felt strange, but man, she needed to wash this day away.

Quickly, she stripped and stepped under the stream. As the warm water hit her back, she closed her eyes, something akin to dread souring her belly. But that dread had nothing to do with her stalker and everything to do with the limited time she had left here in Fallen Ridge.

How was it that she'd met the man less than a week ago, and already she didn't feel capable of leaving him? Hell, they'd spent most of their time together fighting. But even fighting with Nixon felt better than being without him.

She sighed, trying to push aside the dismay of leaving him.

It was fine. She'd done hard before—she could do it again by saying goodbye to Nixon.

She stayed in the shower so long that her fingers wrinkled and the air thickened with steam. When she finally stepped out, she grabbed a towel and wrapped it around her body. She'd just stepped back into her room when the knock sounded at the connecting door. She paused, for a moment wondering whether she should put clothes on first. But why? The man had seen her in less than this.

"Come in."

The door opened, and Nixon immediately stilled. Then, slowly, his gaze trailed down her body, eyes darkening before returning to her face.

Her skin tingled. Any other man and she'd probably hate such a blatant inspection of her body. But with him, it felt good. She liked Nixon's eyes on her. Hell, his gaze felt so intimate, she could almost convince herself he was touching her.

When the silence stretched, she wanted to squirm. "Is everything okay?"

"I was wondering if you wanted to go downstairs and grab something to eat at the bar."

Her brows rose. She hadn't been expecting that. In her head, she'd already planned a night of room service and Netflix in bed. But dinner with this man? Yeah, that was better.

"Sure."

* * *

HOW THE WOMAN was so gorgeous, Nixon had no fucking idea. They were finished with their meals, but he'd barely tasted it. He hadn't paid attention to anything but her all night.

He'd been so damn angry all day. That this woman was the target of some sick fuck. That the asshole had been watching them last night, and Nixon had been so distracted by her and their kiss, he hadn't seen the threat. If the guy had had a gun, it would have been so damn easy to hurt them—or kill them.

He'd been obsessing about it all. Damn. Day. He'd needed to get out of his hotel room before he lost his mind. But he'd also needed to be close to her, and not just because she had a stalker.

Sitting here with her, listening to her speak, watching her smile...it was the closest he'd gotten to peace in hours.

Finley watched the dance floor with a smile. "Look at that couple. They look so happy."

He turned his head to see a man and woman swaying together. They both had graying hair and looked to be maybe in their seventies. He had an arm around her waist and held her hand with his other. They looked like they'd danced together a hundred times before.

Finley sighed. "I wonder how long they've been together."

He looked back at her, seeing longing on her face. She wanted that. "Have you ever come close?"

Her gaze swung back to him, brows rising. "To marriage?" She laughed. "Uh, no. I've always been very career driven. When I was in college, that was my entire focus, and the second my social media platforms started taking off, I turned it into a business and put all my time into building it up. I think I'm a bit too intense for most guys."

Men didn't like her intensity? Fuck, he loved it. The fact that she fought him on everything and had a mind of her own. He'd lived for it these last few days. Her fire. Her passion…it was sexy as hell. "Then those guys aren't for you."

She cocked her head, a ghost of a smile on her lips. "So the problem was them, not me?"

"Yes." Hell yes.

Just the idea of this woman with another man caused anger to ripple through his limbs. He kept that anger locked down and off his face, though, not wanting Finley to see just how much it affected him.

"That makes me feel better." Once again, that look of longing crossed her face as she turned back toward the couple.

Suddenly, he wanted to hold her. To feel her moving in his arms. It hit him so hard, he almost keeled over. "Dance with me." The words were out before he could stop himself. But he didn't regret them or try to tug them back.

Her head snapped back in his direction. "What?"

"Dance with me." Before she responded, he was up and holding out his hand.

She swallowed, her chest heaving on a breath, then she slipped her small, delicate hand into his. "Okay."

The second he was touching her, a weight lifted from his chest.

He led her out to the dance floor, right beside the elderly couple, and pulled her against him, an arm sliding around her waist, the other clasping her hand. They were so close that she was all he could feel. He wanted to fucking bathe in her. To pause this moment and keep her here forever. There were so many lines he was crossing on this trip, but at some point, he'd stopped caring. *This woman* made him stop caring about anything but her.

"I'm glad it was you," she said softly.

Nixon frowned, gaze colliding with her brown eyes. "What?"

"I'm glad it was you—the person Nate hired."

The idea of anyone else protecting her, being where he was

now, made a wildfire of jealousy spread through his veins. No. It was him. Only him.

She smoothed a crease on the material of his shirt. "Can I ask you something?"

His chest tightened, and he had no idea why. Maybe because of the hesitation in her voice or the way she looked at him like she was stripping him bare and seeing every crevice of his soul. "Sure."

"It was Christmas when it happened, wasn't it?"

For a moment, Nixon's world blackened, and he had to remind himself to breathe. To cycle air in and out of his chest. The only thing that kept him upright, the only thing that kept him moving, was her. The way her thumb grazed the back of his hand. The way her eyes bore into his.

"Yes." One word that held so much pain. One word that crushed him. "It was Christmas morning. My parents had gone to pick up my grandparents from the airport. Amy and I wanted to stay home. I was in my room, playing a new video game I'd gotten that morning. The music playing through my headphones was loud."

Agony cut across Finley's features, and tears built in her eyes. "Oh, Nixon… I'm so sorry."

"I was there," he whispered. "But I didn't save her."

"You didn't know she *needed* saving. And you were a child. It wasn't your job."

He wanted to believe her. Fuck, he wanted her words, her touch, to seep inside him and heal every wound he'd ever had.

Like she heard his thoughts, she pulled her hand out of his and brought it up to cup his cheek. "You've been fighting evil your entire adult life to try to make up for the past. But it won't change anything. The healing needs to happen *inside* you. You need to forgive yourself."

"How?" The word was thick and gravelly. "How do you forgive yourself when there's no refuge from the pain?"

She swallowed. "You remind yourself every day that you were a child, that there was nothing you could have done, and you grant yourself peace. You remind yourself that you are a good person and that you'll be okay."

Her words cut to the bone. How did she do that? Dig so deeply inside him and find a way to crumble the walls that had been built so long ago? Walls meant to keep people out and the pain in.

"When I'm with you, I feel like I *might* just be okay." They were words from somewhere deep inside him, and they fell out into the air like small explosives.

Her hand curved into his hair, a small smile turning her lips. "Good. Then I'd better not leave."

The idea of this woman leaving him...it made him tighten his hand on her waist and tug her that bit closer. "No. You'd better not."

CHAPTER 14

Finley inched closer to Nixon. It was busy today, and even though they'd only come for a short amount of time to get a bit of footage, all she wanted to do was go back to the resort. Spend more time alone with Nixon.

They hadn't spoken about what would happen when this trip was over. Sure, he'd said he didn't want to leave her while they'd danced last night, but there were no concrete plans in place.

She wanted to speak to him about it. Hell, when she'd been in his arms last night, those very words had been crawling up her throat, clawing to break free.

But fear had kept them inside her. Fear that she'd push him away with her eagerness. Lose him. But if she didn't ask, she'd never know.

He'd been different today. Quieter, but also…softer. His hand had barely left the small of her back, and she'd felt the soothing rub of his thumb more than once.

She cleared her throat, peeking up at him. "Are you looking forward to going back to Seattle?"

He lifted a shoulder. "I guess so."

"Do you have any pets waiting for you?"

"Nope. I travel too much for that. It wouldn't be fair to them."

She nodded. "I'm the same. I always wanted to get an American pit bull terrier, but at this point in my life, that wouldn't be fair. It wouldn't be fair on the Hunters either, because it would be them I'd ask to look after him on each trip."

"Why a pit bull?"

"I once read that they're the most common type of dog in shelters in the US. It made me sad, and I thought if I just adopted one of them, I'd be doing my part."

When he didn't respond, she looked up to see his brows slashed together as he looked down at her.

"What?" she asked when she couldn't take it anymore.

"You just surprise me."

"Good surprises?"

His lips twitched. "Maybe one day you'll get your pit bull."

Was he avoiding her question? "Hopefully."

When Beth stepped out of the trailer, her eyes immediately found them through the crowd. She beelined toward them, clipboard in hand.

"Hey." She stopped in front of Finley, eyes softening as they ran over her. "How's everything going?"

"Good. No issues at all."

Maybe because of all the security. The place was crawling with new men. She didn't know where Beth had found them, but they were all big and strong and looked ridiculously serious.

Relief washed over the woman's features. "Oh, good."

"I'd like to talk to whichever security guard is in charge," Nixon said.

"Of course. Come." Beth led them to the fair entrance, a few feet from the bridge, where one of the security guards stood. He was as big as Nixon, and there wasn't even a hint of a smile on his face.

God, the two of them could be brothers.

"Nixon, this is Dexter. Dexter, this is Nixon, Finley's bodyguard. He has some questions for you." When her phone beeped, she lifted it and cringed. "Sorry, emergency at the snowman-building station. I'll be back."

Nixon nodded, then turned to Dexter. As the two men talked security, Finley's gaze roamed over the fair.

There were so many people here today. It was hard to believe it was the fair's first year in operation. But then, Beth and Rad seemed to be good at their jobs and motivated to make the fair a success.

She was about to turn back to Nixon when a small girl caught her attention. She was standing on her own by the frozen lake, crying. Finley frowned. The girl looked to be maybe four or five—too young to be by herself. Where was her mother?

Finley scanned the area, but she couldn't see anyone who looked to be searching for a child.

She turned back to Nixon, who was still deep in conversation. It was fine. The girl wasn't far. If Nixon looked for her, she'd be within his sight.

Finley walked forward and crouched next to the child. "Hey. I'm Finley. Are you okay?"

The girl sniffed, tears falling in a steady stream from her eyes. "I can't find my mommy!"

"I'll help you." She held out her hand, and the girl slipped it into hers. "What's your name?"

"Lydia."

"It's nice to meet you, Lydia. Is your mom by herself?"

She shook her head. "No, she's pushing a stroller with my baby brother in it."

"Do you know what color clothing she's wearing?"

Lydia wrinkled her nose. "Um. A purple jacket. It's long and reaches her knees."

"That's good. What about hair color?"

"It's brown. Mommy says we have the same hair."

"Well, she must have beautiful hair then, because your hair is very pretty."

She got a small smile for that.

Finley stood and searched for a woman in a purple jacket pushing a stroller. She walked the girl along the water's edge. When she saw a stroller, she got her hopes up, but the woman's jacket was black. Finley was just about to turn when a woman in purple stepped through the crowd. She was behind a stroller and searching the area frantically, like she'd lost something...or someone.

Finley lowered to her haunches again and pointed. "Is that your mom, Lydia?"

The girl's eyes widened right as the woman spotted them, relief moving over her face. Lydia ran to her mother, while Finley rose and crossed the distance.

"Oh, baby, I thought I lost you!" the woman said, lifting the small girl and kissing her head.

"I was sad. But Finley helped me find you."

The woman looked over her daughter's head. "You helped her?"

"I just walked with her to help her find you."

She reached out and squeezed Finley's arm. "Thank you!"

"You're welcome. Enjoy the fair." Finley gave them one last smile before turning and walking back toward the entrance. She was still smiling, so caught up in her own bubble that she didn't realize how close she'd gotten to the edge of the lake—until a shoulder hit hers, *hard*. She screamed and threw her arms out to catch herself, but there was nothing to grab onto.

The second her body hit the ice, it shattered beneath her, and she was submerged in the frigid water.

Cold blasted her system like a thousand knives pricking her skin, cutting into her. She barely stopped from gasping, knowing the inhalation of water could drown her.

She tried to swim, but God, it was hard! Every limb shook as the combination of cold and panic tried to halt her movements. Take control and render her still.

She forced her foggy mind to work. To reach up for freedom.

But instead of hitting air, her fingers hit ice.

Oh God! Where was the hole she'd broken in the ice?

The panic intensified, her heart thudding against her ribs as her body screamed at her to take a breath. She tried to move her arm, to hit the layer of ice even while looking for the hole, but already her body was shutting down, her limbs refusing to move.

Her vision was going dark when fingers wrapped around her wrist and tugged her forward, then up and out of the water.

* * *

A VEIN THROBBED VIOLENTLY in Nixon's temple. He'd never moved so goddamn fast in his life to get Finley to the car and turn the heat on.

Even with the blanket around her, she shook so violently he could hear her teeth chattering together. Her lips were blue and her skin too pale.

She needed to get out of her wet clothes before hypothermia kicked in, if it hadn't already.

He tried turning the heat up again, only to realize it was already at full capacity.

He wanted to kick his own ass for losing sight of her. It had only been for a moment, while he'd been talking to the guard about her security, but that's all it had taken. One second, she was talking to a small child nearby—the next she was gone.

The panic had been like a living, breathing beast inside him as he searched the crowd. The second he'd heard the scream followed by the ice breaking, he'd known it was her. He had no idea how it happened, but in that moment, it didn't matter. All he'd cared about was getting her out of that water.

When she tried to pull the blanket up but her fingers trembled too violently to grab it, he cursed, pressing his foot harder to the gas.

"Are we going to the h-hotel?" she asked, barely getting the words out.

His teeth clenched together. "No. The hospital."

She shook her head. "No. I d-don't need that. I j-just need to get warm."

"You need a damn hospital, Finley. You would have gone into shock the second you hit the water, and you're too cold."

She grabbed his arm, her fingers like ice. "P-please, Nixon! I h-hate hospitals."

His jaw ground together. The resort *was* closer. "Fine. But if you don't improve quickly, I'm calling an ambulance."

She nodded but remained silent, pulling her arm back under the blanket.

The second he pulled into the resort parking lot, he ran around the car and lifted her out, tugging her against his chest. He jogged inside the resort to the elevator, then stabbed the button three times. It took too damn long for the doors to open.

When he finally stepped inside, Finley nuzzled closer to his chest, digging her face into him, trying to find warmth.

His arms tightened.

His fault. This was *his* fucking fault. The words kept repeating in his head like a damn mantra. He was her protector. And today, he'd failed her—again.

When they finally reached his room, he moved straight to the bathroom to sit her on the edge of the bath. He rose and turned the shower on. He wanted to make it hot for her but knew the water needed to be lukewarm to avoid sending blood away from her heart, then he could gradually heat it up once she was warmer.

He turned back to her and went to his knees. "We need to get these wet clothes off you."

She nodded, skin too pale. She tried to grab the hem of her

top, but her fingers still trembled too violently for her to fully grab the material.

He forced his voice to lower and gentle. "Arms up for me, honey."

For a moment, she met his gaze, teeth still chattering, lips still blue. Then, slowly, she lifted her arms. Nixon peeled the wet material of her sweatshirt and top from her skin, trying not to look at the lacy red bra that barely covered her breasts.

Next, his hands went to her jeans, where he made quick work of the button and zipper.

He met her gaze again. "Lift for me, honey?"

She moved her hands to the tub and pushed up a fraction so he could shift the material down her thighs. Once she was in just her bra and panties, he tugged off his own shirt.

Finley still shook, but now her lips parted, eyes on his chest.

He rose and unbuckled his jeans, then shoved them down so that all he wore were briefs. Then he lifted her into his arms, not missing the small gasp from her lips. She recovered quickly, legs hugging his waist and arms around his neck.

Fuck, she was ice cold.

"This is gonna feel hot," he said gruffly.

She nodded, digging her head into his chest. There was a loud inhale from her as he stepped into the stream of water, her fingers digging into his skin.

He tightened his arms around her. "Are you okay?"

She nodded quickly but remained silent.

He positioned them so the water fell over her body. Every minute that passed had her trembles lessening and the panic in his chest receding. He was still mad as hell, mostly at himself, but if she recovered, he could grant himself just a bit of grace.

When the shaking finally subsided, she lifted her head, her gaze colliding with his. "Thank you. If you hadn't pulled me out—"

"I'll always pull you out." He couldn't even let his mind

consider the alternative. He shifted some hair from her face, gaze focusing on the lips that were no longer blue and the skin that finally had color again. "What happened out there?"

"I was so distracted by the little girl and so happy we found her mom, that I wasn't watching where I was going. I must have walked straight into someone's shoulder."

A vein throbbed in his temple. "Must have?"

"Well, I didn't realize how close I'd gotten to the edge, and then there was a shoulder that bumped into mine..."

Anger, instant and hot, pumped through his blood, roaring between his ears. So some asshole had *knocked* her into the water?

Where the fuck had that person been when she'd fallen in? In fact, a crowd had formed around the water, but not a single goddamn person had done a thing to help her.

"Hey." She pressed a palm to his cheek, drawing him back to her. "I'm okay. You got me out."

"It never should have happened. Not on my watch."

"I walked away. It was my fault." Her gaze shifted between his eyes. Then her head dipped forward, her breath brushing his lips as she whispered. "I'm here. I'm okay. Because of you."

He couldn't stop himself. His mouth crashed to hers, and for the first time since he'd almost lost her, he felt just a semblance of peace.

CHAPTER 15

Finley moaned into the kiss, letting it sink into her chest and heat every crevice that was still cold.

Just like every other time this man had kissed her, his mouth on hers chased away reality, creating a new place just for them. Somewhere quiet and dark and safe.

She smoothed her fingers over his shoulder and up his neck, then into his hair. So soft…his hair and his lips were in complete contrast to the hardness of the rest of him.

When the tiled wall hit her back, she gasped, and he slid inside her mouth, his tongue entwining with hers.

The taste of this man had become so familiar. Like he'd kissed her a thousand times.

"I shouldn't touch you right now," he whispered, voice deep and rough.

She nipped his bottom lip with her teeth, then ran her tongue over it. Teasing. Playing. "You should."

If there was anything that felt right, it was this moment. The two of them connected so intimately.

"You fell into an icy river."

She tugged her mouth from his and trailed kisses across his

cheek before reaching his ear and tugging at the lobe with her teeth. "And you are the only thing making me feel okay right now, so don't you dare stop."

He leaned back, studying her. "It's not just today that I'm talking about… I'm not a safe bet, Finley."

"I don't want safe. I've never wanted safe. I want to *feel* something. And you make me feel everything."

He swallowed. "Some days I can barely keep my head above water."

"Yet today, you were the one pulling me up." She cupped his cheek, letting the pad of her thumb brush his face. "You're stronger than you think. And if you want me, let yourself have me. Because I want *you*. All of you. Even the parts you try to keep hidden."

His eyes darkened, his chest rising and falling on a deep breath. Then his mouth was back on hers, but this kiss was deeper. More desperate. It was his tongue taking over. His body pressing her to the wall, caging her.

She drowned in that kiss. Lost herself and begged to never be found.

When his hands slipped behind her back, she arched, giving him more space as he unhooked her bra. There was the soft thud of material hitting the shower floor, then his hands covered her exposed breasts.

She whimpered as he palmed the soft mounds, the sensations rolling down her body one after the other. When his thumbs found her pebbled nipples, she jolted, his name slipping from her mouth in a whisper as he rolled them.

His mouth moved down her cheek, then neck, before taking one nipple between his lips and sucking. Her back bowed, a cry she couldn't stop tearing from her chest, splintering into the air.

He teased and nipped her hard peak, his hand never leaving her other breast as he rolled her nipple between his thumb and forefinger. Almost involuntarily, she started grinding against him, seeking more. Seeking to dull the throbbing ache in her lower abdomen.

"Nixon. I need you!" She wasn't sure if her words sounded more desperate or pained, and she didn't care. All that mattered was having this man.

When the water turned off, cool air shifted across her wet body as Nixon stepped out of the shower. His mouth returned to hers, and she felt a towel wrap around her back. Then he was moving again until a mattress dipped beneath her back. Gently, he leaned over her, his bare chest pressing against her own.

He was all she could feel.

Grazing her fingers down his chest, she touched every inch of him before slipping a hand inside his briefs. When she wrapped her fingers around him, his body stilled, muscles tensing. Immediately, he grew larger in her hold. She moved her hand, gliding it over his cock, learning what he liked by the growls he released above her.

She moved from base to tip until his fingers suddenly wrapped around her wrist, halting her too soon, and she wanted to protest. But then he was moving down her body, kissing her and sucking a tight nipple as he passed, before stopping with his mouth above the apex of her thighs.

Her breath caught as his fingers slid into the waistband of her panties. Then, torturously slowly, he shuffled the wet material down her thighs and ankles before dropping it to the floor.

When he returned to her, he spread her thighs wide and dipped his head. The second his tongue ran over her clit, her body shuddered violently, her thighs trying to snap together. They met the resistance of his arms and shoulders.

He swiped her again, and this time she cried out, grabbing his hair as his mouth closed over her clit. The man continued to lick and play with her until she was a trembling mess. Until she needed him so desperately that she was sure she'd die or something equally devastating would happen if he didn't return to her.

When a finger went to her entrance, her heart thudded as though the thing was trying to break free. Then he pushed inside her.

"So fucking wet for me," he growled.

She groaned as he pulled out. He started a steady stream of slow thrusts. His mouth returned to her clit once more, alternating between circular motions of his tongue and sucks.

"Nixon…please." She wasn't above begging. At this point, she was willing to do whatever it took to have him inside her. To feel his body between her thighs.

One more thrust of his finger, and finally he lifted, his mouth taking hers for another soul-destroying kiss before he reached for his wallet on the side table and pulled out a foil packet. She watched as he tore it open with his teeth, then removed his briefs and slid the condom over his cock.

Her mouth went dry. So beautiful. Every inch of him. And right now, he was hers.

* * *

BLOOD ROARED between Nixon's ears at the look on Finley's face. Like she had all the trust in the fucking world in him.

Slowly, he returned to her, covering her body with his own, positioning his tip at her entrance. Immediately, she widened for him, wrapping her legs around his waist.

Every part of him begged to push inside her. Take her. But he locked his body, forcing himself to be patient as he cupped her cheek. "You undo me, Finley."

Her expression softened, fingers grazing up his chest and around his neck. She tugged his head down until his lips hovered over hers. "So take me, Nixon. I'm yours."

Then she kissed him as she tightened her legs, bringing him inside her. He groaned deep in his throat, the muscles in his forearms contracting. He slid in deeper, the sound of her moan slipping into his chest and drowning him.

He lifted his hips and thrust back in, feeling the world around him fade. The tatters of everything he knew before her disintegrating until she was all he had and all he needed.

Her head flew back. "Nixon!"

Fuck, he loved hearing his name on this woman's lips. No one said it like she did. It made every territorial part of him scream *mine*.

He thrust faster, harder. Her fingers dug into his skin, carving new marks. Every sound she made, every whimper and whisper, drove him crazy. He wanted to bottle it up to indulge in later, again and again.

When her eyes scrunched, all he could do was watch. Get so fucking lost in her, he didn't want to be found.

He lowered his head and latched his mouth to her neck—sucking, tasting, claiming.

With his free hand, he found her pebbled nipple, and he rolled it between his thumb and forefinger, loving the sounds the action drew from her. The shudders that rolled down her body.

His. She was fucking *his*.

The thought was so loud in his head that it was all he heard. He'd never wanted another person as his own before, but here, with Finley, *inside* Finley, he felt it. He felt it so fucking strongly, it wiped out every reason he had *not* to claim her.

When she tugged his head back to her, he rose and found her mouth again, his thrusts never stopping. The woman tasted like honey, soft and sweet. He let his tongue duel with hers as he lifted her thigh, pumping into her at a new angle. His heart thudded so hard in his chest that he could hear it.

Releasing her thigh, he reached down and swiped her clit. She cried out. He did it again, used his thumb to apply pressure, moving in a circular motion.

Suddenly, her walls tightened around him and she shattered,

her scream slicing through the room. Her nails dug into his shoulders, nearly breaking skin.

He welcomed the lick of pain. The deafening screams. He kept pumping. Kept moving until finally, his own body tensed and he broke, giving everything he was and had to this woman, until he had nothing left.

When he finally stilled, there was only the thumping of their hearts. The quick rush of breaths.

He touched his forehead to hers, needing every little connection he could get. Needing all of Finley.

Her hands came up to cradle the sides of his head. "Nixon... that was..."

"Something else," he finished when she couldn't.

She nodded. "Something else."

It was something deep and important. Something that changed *everything*.

Slowly, he pulled out of her and rolled to the side, tugging her into him. "I should feed you."

She shook her head. "Not yet. Right now I just need *you*."

He closed his eyes, letting her words wash over him. Twist his insides.

And yet again, those words whispered inside his head. That she was his. Not just for now. Not just for this trip. Always. And fuck, that scared the shit out of him.

CHAPTER 16

*N*ixon stroked a hand down Finley's back. The sun had been up for a while, its rays slipping through the cracks in the curtains and shining over the bed sheets. But Finley hadn't so much as stirred. Which meant he had time to just hold her. Watch the slow rise and fall of her chest. Listen to the gentle wisps of air moving between her lips.

He was trying to remain calm. Hell, he was doing everything in his power to remind himself that he shouldn't run from this. That whatever was happening between them was okay.

He'd never felt like this for a woman before. He'd always thought that was because he hadn't allowed himself to feel anything. To have something to lose. Something to protect.

But on this trip, he was learning none of that was a choice. At least, not with Finley.

When her thumb grazed his stomach, he looked down to see her eyes scrunching. The rhythm of her breaths changed from long, deep inhalations to short, shallow ones. Then, slowly, her eyes opened, and she looked at him.

A smile curved her lips, and it was like a kick to the gut. Fuck, she was beautiful. And right now, hair mussed, completely bare as she lay half sprawled across him, every territorial instinct inside him sprang to life.

"Hey," she whispered.

He brushed some hair from her face. "Hey, beautiful."

The smile softened. "Have you been awake for a while?"

"Nah." A damn lie. He'd been awake long enough to memorize every little sound this woman made while she slept. Every flicker of movement she made down to the rhythm of her chest.

She swallowed, fingers brushing his skin. "Last night was…amazing."

"*You're* amazing."

She tilted her head. "You're not gonna turn around and be a jerk again, are you?"

His lips twitched. "You think I was a jerk?"

"I know you were. And you know you were, too."

He bit back a chuckle at the adamance in her voice. Yeah, he *had* been a jerk. But to be fair, he was that way to everyone. "No, Fin. I'm not gonna turn around and be a jerk."

The air whooshed out of her. "Thank God." Then, she pushed up so that her mouth hovered over his. "That means I can kiss you."

"You can still kiss me when I'm being a jerk."

"I know." Her breath brushed over his face. "But you don't deserve it then."

She lowered her mouth and touched his lips. And there it was again. The feeling that she was his. That he couldn't be without her. It plagued him. Tormented him.

He deepened the kiss, tasting the woman. She hummed, and the sound turned his chest into a tattered mess.

Immediately, he flipped them, pressing her into the mattress and smoothing his hand up her side. He was about to cup her breast when his phone rang from the bedside table. He wanted to ignore it—hell, he was *going* to ignore it—but Finley took her mouth from his and touched their foreheads.

"You should answer that," she breathed.

No, he fucking shouldn't.

"I should get dressed anyway," she continued, her fingers dusting across his shoulders. "So we can go to the Christmas fair before it gets busy."

The muscles in Nixon's forearms flexed. "You think we're gonna go to the fair after you almost died yesterday?"

There was a bite to his words, but he couldn't help it. She'd been pushed into the goddamn water. If he'd pulled her out a couple minutes later, if he hadn't heard her go in, she probably wouldn't be here right now.

His phone stopped ringing as her brows tugged together. "Yes, I am. I need to get footage of the tobogganing. It's in my contract."

"No." The word was out before he could stop it. "You've been there every damn day since this thing started. You've done your job."

Determination narrowed her eyes, and she shoved at his chest. He didn't move an inch.

"Finley—"

"Get off, Nixon. I'm going to my room to change."

The anger that pressed at his chest nearly choked him.

Another shove, and he finally leaned to the side to let her up. She climbed to her feet and grabbed his discarded shirt from the floor before tugging it over her head.

"It's too dangerous," he growled.

She spun back to face him. "You still don't get it. My job is all I have! I've put everything into making it what it is. I don't have rich parents to fall back on if I fail. I'm it. And I will finish what I've signed on to do."

"At what cost? Your life? Because that's what this asshole wants."

For a fleeting second, fear flickered through her eyes. Then she blinked. "What happened was my fault. I got too close to the edge. I was distracted and bumped into someone's shoulder."

He scoffed. "That's bullshit and you know it."

She planted her fists on her hips. "This is *my* life, Nixon. I put it out there for the world to see. And if you can't handle that…"

When she trailed off, his jaw clicked. "If I can't handle that, maybe we shouldn't be doing this? Is that what you're saying?"

Her throat bobbed, and she avoided his eyes. When she spoke again, her tone was resigned. "I'm going to get ready. You should return that call. Today's my last day at the fair, and it's Christmas in two days. We can hide out until the flight, but today, I have to go."

She didn't wait for him to respond, just slipped out of his room and back into hers. The sound of the door thudding shut was like a kick in the gut.

The cell rang again.

"Yeah?"

There was a small beat of silence, then Nate spoke. "Hey. Everything okay?"

No. It was about as far as it fucking got from okay. "It's fine. What do you need?"

"My mission took less time than I thought it would, so I'm trying to call Finley but can't get through. The calls keep going to voicemail. Is everything all right?"

Shit. Her phone. It was probably in her pocket when she fell through the ice yesterday. Would she even have a device to get footage today? "She fell into some water. It probably broke."

There was a weighty pause. "*Water?* What kind of water?"

"An icy lake." Nate cursed as Nixon continued, "She's okay. I pulled her out."

"How'd she end up in the damn water?"

"We don't know. She thinks she got too close to the edge and bumped into someone. I disagree."

"Goddammit. The quicker this trip is over, the better."

"Yeah." That was all he had…a "yeah." Because what happened after the trip?

He ran a frustrated hand through his hair.

"Everything going okay between you two?" Nate asked, like he somehow knew it wasn't.

"Yep." Another damn lie.

There was yet another pause, and when his friend spoke again, his voice held a warning. "Nix—what's going on?"

"We got together."

Nate cursed again, this time louder. But when he spoke, his voice was low. *"How?* You don't date. You've told me that numerous times. Hell, I've seen it. You hook up with women, but that's it. So what is this? A fling?"

Nixon's back teeth ground together. "Nate—"

"She's important to me, Nixon. You know that. So don't fuck around with her. You need to be a hundred percent on this. You need to know that you can handle her life—that you can handle *her*—long term."

* * *

Finley tried not to tap her foot on the floor of the car. It was a nervous habit of hers.

When she'd knocked on Nixon's door, he'd opened it with that familiar closed-off expression on his face again.

She hated that look. The second she'd seen it, it felt like all their progress had just disappeared. Hell, it felt like last night had never happened.

"Wait for me to come around," he said in a low, hard tone when they pulled into the fair lot.

Before she could respond, he was out.

To distract herself, she pulled out her backup phone. Thank God she'd brought it. She usually did, just in case, because of how dependent her job was on access to both a camera and her social media accounts. But this was the first time she'd actually had to use it.

When her door opened, she climbed out. He set a hand on the small of her back, but there was nothing intimate about his touch. He was all business today.

She sighed. "Nixon, I don't want to fight."

"We're not fighting."

She almost rolled her eyes. "Okay, what would you call this?"

"Work. You're doing your job, and I'm doing mine."

She tried not to flinch. Was he talking about just this moment or more than that? It felt like more. It almost felt like he was telling her *everything* had been just work.

They were halfway to the toboggans when Beth and Rad walked past. They were deep in conversation, but when Beth noticed Finley, her expression was one of concern.

She rushed over to them and touched her arm. "Hey! Are you okay? I tried to call you yesterday but couldn't get through. I was so worried."

"Sorry, my phone was in my pocket and isn't working now. But I'm okay. Nixon got me back to the resort and got me warm."

Beth pressed a hand to her chest. "Thank God."

"How'd it happen?" Rad asked, looking far less concerned than Beth.

"I was distracted and bumped into someone. It was my fault. I'm sorry to have caused a scene."

"Oh my gosh, don't apologize," Beth rushed out before Rad could respond. "That must have been so traumatic. I can't even imagine falling through ice. I'm surprised you're here instead of taking a day off. Tobogganing footage, right?"

Nixon tensed beside her.

She swallowed. "I wanted to come and get one last bit of footage."

"So, it's your last day?"

She nodded.

"Well, I need to thank you now, then, don't I?" She wrapped Finley in a hug. "Thank you for helping us make this fair a success."

Finley returned the hug. "All I did was post about my time here."

Beth pulled back, squeezing Finley's shoulders. "You created engaging content, blasted it out to your fans, and have brought people in droves. Thank you. Have a lovely Christmas."

She squeezed her shoulders once more before linking an arm through Rad's. He dipped his chin, heading off with his cousin.

As Finley continued forward, she couldn't help but feel a bit lighter. There had been real gratitude in the woman's eyes. She'd made a small difference for them and what they were doing here. It felt good.

When they reached the tobogganing station, she grabbed a sled. Nixon tried to take it from her, but she shook her head. "I'll carry it. You keep your hands free in case you need to get all badass bodyguard."

He just nodded. God, she didn't even get a smile? A small twitch of his lips?

With a sigh, she started toward the hill, then stopped behind the long line of people who were waiting to go down. As they stood together quietly, she took a couple videos of the hill itself, as well as the line in front of her.

When they were halfway through the queue, she couldn't take the silence anymore. She spun on him. "This is about more than me coming today, isn't it?"

His gaze remained on anything and everything but her. "I don't know what you're talking about."

Oh man, she'd never wanted to slap a person in her life, but right now, that was exactly what she wanted to do, just to get some damn emotion out of him. "Are you having second thoughts about us?"

His jaw clenched. And when his silence lengthened, her chest cracked.

He was.

It may have only been one night together, but it meant something to her, and she'd thought it meant something to him too. Thought it cemented them together.

She forced the hurt and devastation off her face as they moved forward with the line. "Do you wish last night never happened?"

A pained look came over his face. "Finley…"

"Do you?"

Another silence that was so damn loud it made her belly coil with nausea.

Her breaths started to shorten. "You do, don't you?"

"I'm not a relationship guy."

Tears pricked at her eyes, but she blinked them away. "You could be. You *choose* not to be. And you know what? I am not going to force you to see my worth."

She wanted to. She wanted to do everything possible to make this man want to keep her. But she shouldn't have to.

When the line moved forward, Finley forced a smile to her lips as she walked up to one of the employees working the hill. "Hi. I was wondering if you could film me going down for my socials?"

The girl's eyes widened. "Oh my gosh—you're Finley. I follow you on TikTok and Instagram."

"I am."

"Of course I will. God, I'm going to be taking footage for Finley freaking Dunkley! That's crazy!"

It took too much energy to keep the smile in place. "Thank you."

Nixon stood beside her, his gaze forever scanning the area.

She lowered to the toboggan. When Nixon didn't sit behind her, she frowned. "Are you coming?"

"I'm gonna watch you go down." His hand hovered near his concealed holster, his gaze moving around the hill.

There were half a dozen others at the top of the slope. She doubted someone would attack her here. But even if they might, she didn't have the energy to argue.

With a deep sigh and a shake of her head, she pushed off the edge of the hill. Cold air lashed her face as the sled glided over the snow.

She was halfway down when someone careened into her from behind.

She gasped, her head whipping back as she was sent off course.

Voices shouted from behind her, and she looked up to see a tree stump. She couldn't avoid the collision.

The hit knocked the air from her lungs—then she was airborne before her head hit something hard upon landing.

The pain was instant, darkness blurring her vision.

There was movement around her. Voices. But they sounded far away.

Then Nixon's voice. "Fin! Honey, talk to me!"

She opened her mouth, but no words came out. Then darkness closed in around her.

CHAPTER 17

Other than the slow rise and fall of Finley's chest, she was completely still. Fuck, he hated it. He hated that she looked so pale and small in the hospital bed. That yet again, she'd been placed in danger today. That she'd been hurt.

His jaw clenched and it was an effort to remain where he was. To not get up and yell or hit something.

Someone had crashed straight into her toboggan. No one realized that the sledder was heading straight toward her until it was too late.

His heart had damn near stopped. Had it been him? Had his goal been to hurt her without killing her? Because Finley *had* been hurt.

When he couldn't remain seated any longer, he rose and raked his hands through his hair as he paced the small room.

The entire fucking thing had almost unfolded in slow motion, while he'd been unable to do a damn thing to stop it. It had been torture. The hit. The veering of the sled before she hit the tree stump, then the pole. Even now, replaying it in his head killed him.

He'd wanted to go down the hill and find the fucker. Chase

after the asshole and make sure he breathed his last breath. But the need to get to her, to make sure she was okay, had been like a living, breathing thing inside him. Nothing and no one would have stopped him.

Paramedics had taken too long to get to the fair. That's when Nixon had finally watched the phone footage. The person who'd hit her had been a man in a beanie. The footage had been from behind, though, so there'd been nothing distinctive about him.

He'd shown some guards and told them to search the fair, but he'd known it was a wasted endeavor. The fair was packed, there was no finding him.

His phone dinged.

Nate: How is she?

He'd texted Nate about what happened the second they'd reached the hospital. His friend had been angry as hell, but also worried.

Nixon: Confirmed concussion and some bruises, but that's all. I'm just waiting for her to wake up.

Nate: Look after her for us.

Nixon: Already done.

He shoved his phone into his pocket before his gaze returned to Finley. Fuck, he was a mess. His emotions were all over the place. After his conversation with Nate that morning, he'd pulled away from her, the certainty that she was his suddenly wavering. Because Nate had been right, he didn't do relationships. Never had. Was he even capable? He had no idea.

And what if he told her he *could*? What if he got her to uproot her life to be closer to him and she fell in love with him, then he fucked up? Hurt her?

He'd hate himself even more.

He ran a frustrated hand through his hair, pacing up and down the length of the room. Conflicting emotions of pain and guilt and anger rioted inside him.

"Wake up for me, honey," he begged, never taking his eyes off her. "Show me those beautiful brown eyes. Let me know you're okay."

She didn't. She just lay there, so damn still.

When his phone rang, he almost expected it to be Nate again. It was Beth.

"Did you find him?" he growled, unable to smooth out the sharpness of his voice.

"No," she said quietly. "The description was too broad to isolate him. Most of the men here are wearing dark beanies and jackets."

He knew that, but damn, it still hurt.

"It's good today was her last day," Beth said, voice resigned. "I think her being at the fair isn't safe for anyone."

Damn straight it wasn't. "I couldn't agree more, Beth."

She sighed. "Okay. Good. Well, please let her know Rad and I are thinking of her. And let me know if there's anything we can do."

"Thanks. Will do."

When he hung up, he lowered to the seat beside Finley's bed. Unable to stop himself, he lifted her hand and brought it to his lips before pressing a kiss to her skin. The call this morning had shaken his confidence in them. In his ability to take care of her and be what she needed him to be. But after today, after seeing her hurt, and not for the first time…he wasn't capable of walking away.

Maybe he'd screw things up, maybe he wouldn't. But one thing he was absolutely sure of was that he'd do the best he could to be what she needed. Be the best version of himself possible for her. Because he needed her safe, and he needed her in his life.

He kept her hand close to his lips as he whispered, "Come back to me, honey. I need you."

* * *

DREAD POOLED in Finley's belly. That smell...antiseptic and cleaning detergent. So familiar, yet she hated every part of it and the memories it evoked. And it wasn't just the smell. It was the incessant beeping. The tapping of shoes on vinyl flooring.

The rhythm of her heart sped up as her skin chilled. A hospital. She was in a hospital. Why?

She forced herself to think through the fog. She wasn't in Redwood. She was in Fallen Ridge, Ontario, for the Winter Wonderland Christmas Fair. Is that where she'd been hurt?

God, everything was a blur.

She scrunched her eyes, trying to pull back flickers of her last memory. Nixon. She'd been fighting with Nixon. And she'd had a sled because they were on the toboggan slope.

Then what?

Her breaths shortened and she was just spiraling into a deep panic when pressure enclosed her fingers. Warmth.

Then his voice.

"You're safe."

Immediately, the panic dulled, and even though she lay in a hospital bed with no memory of how she got here, she *felt* safe. Because Nixon was here.

Slowly, she peeled her eyes open. Pain immediately pricked at her skull like tiny stabs of a blade. But she pushed through, needing to see him. Needing answers.

The second her gaze collided with his, air she hadn't realized she'd been holding rushed from her chest. He looked tired. Dark circles shadowed his eyes, and thick lines sat between his brows.

But he was here.

"Are you okay?" she whispered.

The frown deepened, the fingers around her hand tightening. "Am *I* okay? No, honey. I'm not. Because you're in a hospital bed."

She swallowed at the reminder. "I hate hospitals. It reminds me of when my dad got sick."

His thumb swiped across the back of her hand.

"I visited him as much as I could when he got sick. It wasn't enough because I was a kid and needed Mom to take me. She didn't care as much as she should have. And now I associate hospitals with watching him fade away."

"I'm sorry you had to go through that."

She breathed through the heavy memories. Then she asked the question she needed an answer to. "Why am I here?"

"You don't remember?"

She shook her head, and pain immediately pinged in her skull.

Nixon saw it. Of course he did. His biceps flexed, fingers tightening around her hand. "Someone crashed into the back of your sled as you were going down the hill. You hit a tree stump, then the fence."

Little flashes of memory trickled back to her. The collision from behind as she was going down the hill. The inability to turn as the tree stump came into view.

So that was the head pain. "Did anyone see the guy who hit me?" A part of her hoped it was an accident. But the bigger part of her knew that was wishful thinking.

Nixon's eyes darkened. "No. People were so focused on you, no one saw the guy. We have footage on your phone but can only see the back of him, and it's not enough to identify him."

Her lips parted, anger twisting her gut. "I am so sick of this person messing with me! He's scared me. Threatened me. Stalked me. And I'm over it! I need him caught and for him to leave me the hell alone!"

"You and me both, Fin." There was the glitter of promise in Nixon's expression, like he'd personally make sure the man was caught. "But today was your last day at the fair, so at least he can't target you there anymore."

"Even if I hadn't decided that, I wouldn't go back. Up until this point, I've been making excuses. Blaming things on accidents. But I need to stop doing that. It's him. It's all him. And I can't go back and risk anyone else at the fair getting hurt."

Today, the guy could have pushed her into someone else's path. She could have hit other people going down the hill, and *they* could have been hurt. God, there had been kids all over the place. If one of them had gotten hurt—

"Hey."

Nixon's voice pulled her away from her spiraling thoughts. He cupped her cheek. "Everyone's okay."

"But if they weren't, it would have been my fault."

"No. It would have been *his*."

Tears she couldn't stop filled her eyes. Tears of anger. Of frustration. "I hate this! I hate that I can't do my job without feeling unsafe. I should be able to live my life without being scared."

"Finley—"

"Why is he doing this? Why won't he leave me alone?"

His thumb grazed her cheek. "He's sick. It has nothing to do with you and everything to do with him. But he *will* be stopped. I promise you—I will personally make sure of it."

His words seeped deep inside her, slowing her racing heart. Calming her.

Gently, like she was made of glass, he leaned in close and held her. She breathed him in, letting his strength and power soothe her.

He was the only thing keeping her from going over the edge. He was her anchor. Her sanctuary. Her safe place.

CHAPTER 18

Finley rolled onto her belly before reaching out a hand, expecting to find Nixon, but instead brushed her fingers over cold sheets. Frowning, she opened her eyes to see his empty hotel room. Her gaze shifted to the closed bathroom door. Water hitting tiles registered next.

She closed her eyes and lay back down, the events of the previous day washing over her for what had to be the hundredth time. After she was released from the hospital, Nixon had brought her back to the hotel and not left her side. He'd been attentive and caring. The complete opposite of how he'd acted just minutes before the incident.

They'd ordered room service and eaten it on the couch while watching some romantic comedy in pajamas. The movie had been her choice, of course, not his. Then she'd fallen asleep on his shoulder and woken during the night to find she was in his bed, in his arms.

He'd woken her every two hours after that, on the doctor's instructions.

Turning her head, she spotted two pills and a glass of water beside the bed. Her pain medication. Anyone would have thought their fight yesterday morning hadn't happened, considering how gentle and sweet he'd been.

Sitting up, she noticed her head didn't actually feel too bad today. There was a dull pain at the back of her skull, but nothing like yesterday. Good.

The shower in the bathroom turned off, and her heart started to thump. It was crazy, but she still got nervous around the guy. Nervous when he looked at her. Touched her.

A minute passed and Nixon stepped out, a towel wrapped low around his waist. And yep, her belly did a dozen little flips. Because God, he was beautiful. Thick cords of muscle. A wide chest. And right now, he had small drops of water running over his skin.

His intense gaze beamed straight to her. "You're awake. How are you feeling?"

"Okay, considering."

When the towel dropped, her mouth went dry. As he tugged on briefs, jeans, and a shirt, she couldn't take her eyes away from him. He was just so…powerful. In every way.

He looked at the pills on her bedside table. "You haven't taken your pain medication."

"It doesn't hurt much today."

His brows flickered and he crossed the space between them. He lifted the pills and touched them to her lips. "You shouldn't push it. I don't want you in any pain."

She opened her mouth. The press of his fingertips against her lips was intoxicating. He slipped her the pills before lifting the glass to her mouth.

"I tried getting us a flight out today, but the earliest they had was tomorrow in the middle of the day," he said quietly.

A Christmas Day flight. She wasn't sure how she felt about that. Not only because of her stalker but because that was the end of this bubble she had with Nixon in Canada.

"Thank you for organizing that," she said softly before

nibbling her bottom lip, debating how to word what she wanted to ask. But hell, there was no easy way to do it, so she just needed to rip off the Band-Aid. "What are we going to do when we get back? About us?"

There was a small flexing of his muscles. She was sure he'd tried to hide it. "I don't know."

Her chest constricted. Because she *wanted* him to know. She wanted him to be as sure about them as she was. If he asked her to, she'd move. She'd pick up her life and rebuild it wherever Nixon needed to be. But he hadn't asked.

She swallowed, heart thumping far too hard and fast in her chest. "Are you wanting to continue this thing between us when we get back to the US?"

He hesitated—and that small pause hurt so much more than it should have. Had the situation been reversed, she wouldn't have needed a second to think about it.

"I should get up." She didn't look at him as she threw off the blankets and rose from the bed.

"Finley…"

She ignored him, crossing into her room and closing the connecting door, not wanting him to see the hurt on her face or the tears building in her eyes.

For a moment, she just stood there, leaning against the wood as she blinked the tears away. Then she stripped off her pajamas and pulled on running tights, a sports bra, and a sweater. She was just putting on her socks and shoes when the connecting door opened.

"Finley—" He stopped, but she didn't look up. "What are you doing? You can't go for a run. You had a concussion yesterday."

"I'm going for a walk."

"No—"

"I need to get out of this room." That was nonnegotiable. When her mind was a mess, when her world felt like it was imploding around her, she needed to move. To be outside. To breathe fresh air. Not be caged indoors.

She rose and stepped around him, making it halfway across the room when strong fingers wrapped around her wrist.

"Finley, I don't think—"

"I do." She pressed a hand to his chest, forcing her gaze up to his deep brown eyes. "I need to go for a walk. You can join me or wait here."

A muscle twitched in his cheek before he slowly released her. Then she was moving again, walking out of the room and down the hall, Nixon behind her. When she stepped into the elevator, it felt too small. She smacked at the button, begging the ride down to go quickly.

Nixon's smell, his closeness, was intoxicating. It pulled her in, and all she wanted to do was lean into his chest. But he didn't want her with the same certainty. The same desperation. And God, that cut across her flesh like a blade.

When she reached the foyer, she was walking out before the doors had fully opened, all but falling outside. She gulped in long breaths of air, letting the cold fill her lungs. Needing it to calm her.

She walked quickly down the path, forcing her legs to pump at a pace she knew was too fast, given her condition last night.

"Finley, slow down."

Not only did she ignore Nixon, she sped up, gulping in more air, desperately hoping her racing heart would disguise that *other* pain in her chest.

"Finley!" When she ignored him again, his fingers wrapped around her arm for a second time that morning, pulling her to a stop. "You need to—"

"Why are you so scared to want me?"

His brows slashed together. "What?"

"Why are you so scared for me to be yours, permanently?"

Emotion flickered in his eyes, so deep and dark, he was

almost unrecognizable. "Because then I have something to lose." His voice held a depth of pain she hadn't anticipated.

Her breath stuttered, her heart cracking at the fear she saw in his eyes. Because there *was* fear. And in a man like Nixon, a man who looked like he could hold the world on his shoulders, that fear was soul-wrenching.

She stepped forward. "But if you push me away, you've lost me anyway."

He ran a hand over his face, something akin to panic there now. "I'm trying to protect myself."

"But at what cost? Losing us? Losing what we could be?" She pressed her hands to his chest, feeling the steady thump of his heart beneath her palm. "I'm falling in love with you, Nixon. Do you feel the same way?"

At his silence, every pain she'd ever felt was a shadow in comparison to this one.

No. He didn't feel the same.

This time, she stepped away from him, but the step was more of a stumble. "I can't keep going in circles like this. My heart can't take it."

* * *

THE DISTANCE she put between them hit like a physical blow to his midsection, so hard and intense it stole his breath. "Finley, I don't want to hurt you."

"You are. By pushing me away, by not allowing yourself to feel anything, you *are* hurting me." She swallowed, a thin sheen of tears in her eyes. "Tell me you don't want me."

Fuck, how was he supposed to respond to that? "Finley—"

"Tell me you don't want me, Nixon."

"I can't. I *do* want you. I want all of you, all the time. I've never wanted anything in my *life* as much as I want you. You're in my skin. My blood. My bones. You're everywhere." The words flew from somewhere deep inside him, and he couldn't stop a single one of them. "And that scares the hell out of me."

More tears built in her beautiful brown eyes. She closed that distance between them again, and the second she touched him, a small fleck of his pain disintegrated. "You have me. Take me as yours."

"You don't know what you're saying."

"I do. I feel the fear too. But there's also a different kind of fear. The fear you feel when something so perfect is in the palm of your hand, but it's slipping through your fingers like sand."

Him. He was the sand.

Her hands smoothed over his chest, and it felt like she was inside him, her fingers around his heart, claiming it. "The only thing worse than fear is regret. Don't let that be us. If you want me, take me."

Her words, the way her breath brushed against his flesh, it caused the last scrap of his resistance to snap. He tugged her against him and took her lips with his.

The kiss was fire, and that fire burned the fear in his chest to ash.

She moaned, softening, her hands running over his chest and shoulders. The sounds she made silenced the world around him. Fuck, they even silenced the voices in his head.

He slid his fingers through her hair, holding her. Needing her.

His. This woman was *his*. He'd tried running. Hell, he'd tried digging his head into the damn dirt and pretending she didn't affect him. But none of that had worked. And now, he needed to stop running. To stop letting fear dictate his whole damn life.

He slipped his tongue between her lips, tasting her. Letting everything that was Finley change him. Claim him.

He didn't know how long they kissed, but when he eventually came up for air, it was too soon. Gently, he touched his forehead to hers. "I wasn't lying when I said I'm not a safe bet. But for you,

I'll try. Fuck, I'll tear myself and my world apart to be what you need. Because I'm falling in love with you, too."

Her eyes closed, relief skittering over her features and a single tear falling down her cheek. He caught it with the pad of his thumb.

"Nixon..." Her eyes collided with his. "Promise me...no more running. We make this work. We figure it out. Together."

"No more running. It's you and me, Finley. Together."

CHAPTER 19

Finley's fingers tapped the keys on her laptop as she responded to emails. She'd been doing admin all afternoon, ever since she and Nixon had returned from their walk.

Her heart was still thudding too quickly at what had transpired between them. At the way he'd kissed her. Admitted to falling in love with her.

She snuck a peek at him. They were on the couch in his room, the heat of his side close to her, almost touching.

He was on his laptop too, although every so often he took a break to kiss her. Touch her.

He almost made her forget everything that had transpired with her stalker. That she'd been in the hospital. Hearing him tell her he wanted to make things work between them… God, it had made all the anxiety she'd been feeling just disappear.

She ran her gaze over the email she'd written, her finger hovering over the send key. It was going to the coordinator of the next event she'd committed to, informing them she could no longer attend. That due to personal reasons, she had to withdraw.

She'd recommended a number of other people who had big followings like hers, who would no doubt take her place if asked.

The email said exactly what she wanted…yet she hesitated, something inside her rebelling at the idea of sending it. She'd never withdrawn from an event once she'd committed. Because every event was one she'd carefully selected.

She needed a break. But she also knew that break would hurt the carefully crafted business she'd created. In her line of work, you couldn't just take time off and return later to where you were before you left.

But then, she couldn't keep going either. Yesterday had been a wake-up call, and honestly, she needed some time to herself. The chance to keep her life private so this kind of thing couldn't repeat itself.

With a long inhale, she clicked send, her heart thumping against her ribs when it disappeared off the screen.

"Hey, you okay?"

She turned to look at Nixon, her gaze colliding with his beautiful eyes. "I just canceled my next job. And even though it feels like the right thing to have done, it also feels…heavy. Like I'm losing something."

He brushed some hair behind her ear. "Of course it does. You've spent years building up your platform, and taking a step back is hard."

Her breath caught at his unexpected words. This entire time, she'd thought he didn't understand what her work meant to her.

"I have," she said quietly. "A lot of people don't understand what I do, and some even think it's not a real job, but it's been hard to get where I am. It's a saturated industry with a lot of people vying for the same events. And the thing about this work is you can lose momentum and be forgotten quickly, then never get back to where you were."

He ran a thumb down her arm. "The work you've put into your job is evident, Finley."

"Thank you for seeing that. As much as I want to keep doing it, though, I need a break, and I need the people around me to be safe. I don't know what I'll do in the meantime, but for a while at least, I need to not be in the spotlight."

"Is there anything else you want to do?"

She nibbled her bottom lip. "There has been something that's been on my mind for a while."

"What?"

"When I was a kid, I wanted to be a teacher, but I didn't think I'd like being confined to a classroom all day." She studied his expression. "I was thinking…maybe I could help others build *their* platforms. Like one-on-one sessions. Or I could even design a course."

One side of Nixon's mouth lifted. "I think that's a great idea."

"Really?"

"Yeah. You can do it from anywhere, no classroom required. And I think you'd be in high demand."

Something bubbled inside her. Little crumbs of excitement at the new path she could embark on.

"And if anyone can make a success out of a career change, it's you." He leaned over and kissed her.

She couldn't stop the beam of a smile. "Thank you."

One more kiss and he leaned back. "Let me know when you're done, and we'll grab something to eat."

"Room service?" She'd basically tried everything on the menu now, and she loved it all.

"Actually, I booked somewhere for dinner."

She frowned, confused. She'd thought he wanted to remain in the room until they left. "Really?"

"Yeah." He lifted a shoulder. "It's Christmas Eve. We're leaving tomorrow. I wanted to do something nice."

God, this man was just full of surprises.

"That sounds wonderful," she said quietly. "I just need to post my final fair content, then we can go."

"Sounds good."

She was still smiling when she looked back at her screen. She'd already edited her footage. It was supposed to have been of her tobogganing. Obviously, there was no way she could post that. So instead, her last content creation for the fair was a mash-up of everything they had to offer. The food and drink, the snowman building and ice-skating. The horse and sleigh rides and general footage of the tobogganing.

The fair would be open for the rest of December, but since she wouldn't be here, this was her last push to get people to attend.

Her smile slipped as she watched the footage. Just about every part of the fair had been tainted by this stalker of hers. She hated him. Hated that she'd been so excited about this job and trip, and a single person had set out to target her and ruin that.

All she could do was hope that he was caught soon, and that she'd never see or hear from him again afterward.

She posted her clips on all her platforms, and even posted a longer fifteen-minute YouTube video on her channel. The second they were up, her followers began interacting with the content.

The old her was always excited about that interaction. Some-times she'd even just sit and watch the comments roll in, completely in awe that it was *her* content people were loving. But now, like the fair, this guy had tainted that. Made her scared of every new subscriber and follower. And all she could do was wait for him to say something to make her skin crawl.

Heat suddenly pressed to her side, then lips to her neck. "You ready for me to take you out to dinner now?"

Immediately, the tension uncoiled from her belly as she leaned into him. "I am. On one condition."

"A condition?" Nixon nipped her skin and she shuddered. "And what condition would that be?"

"You have to try the eggnog."

He groaned, shaking his head. "I don't do eggnog."

She turned, pleading with him with her eyes. "Just a small sip of mine? Please? I guarantee you'll love it."

"I tried it when I was a kid. I did not love it. But if they have eggnog, I'll taste it."

"It's Christmas Eve…they'll have eggnog. And I think your adult tastebuds will be pleasantly surprised."

"One sip." Then his head lowered, and he kissed her again.

* * *

"So…WHAT do you think? Good, huh?"

He swallowed the thick, sweet drink, letting the nutmeg and cinnamon sit heavily in his gut. "It tastes like melted ice cream."

Her eyes lit up. "Yes, it does!"

She said it like that was a good thing. Did people actually want to drink melted ice cream?

He handed back her drink.

"I can order you one if you want." The words were barely out of her mouth before she was looking for a waiter.

"I'm fine with my beer." Not that he'd be drinking much of it. He'd made the dinner reservation earlier today, because even though he didn't like Christmas, she did. And fuck, he wanted to make her happy. He damn well lived for the little rises of the corners of her lips. The small laughs that fell from her mouth.

She sipped her eggnog, gaze shifting around the restaurant. "This place is fancy."

"Is that a good thing or a bad thing?"

She lifted a shoulder. "I like it. But I'm not a girl who needs to be wined and dined. A burger and fries works just as well for me as a piece of salmon."

The truth was, he'd booked here because they had live music and dancing. And watching Finley move on the dance floor, holding her in his arms, was what he needed tonight.

The waitress set their meals onto the table. Finley took a bite of her salmon, her eyes closed, and a groan slipped from her lips. The sound was so fucking sexy that his damn dick twitched.

"Okay, I take it back," she said, eyes still closed. "I do need fancy in my life. Because this is to die for."

She put some more on her fork and held it out for him. He opened his mouth and ate it, but his eyes never left hers.

"Amazing, isn't it?" she asked excitedly.

"Yeah. Amazing." But he wasn't talking about the salmon.

She beamed, turning back to her food. As they ate, they didn't talk much. But then, they didn't need to. With Finley, the silence was comfortable. He was happy to sit and just be with Finley.

When they finally finished, he rose and held out his hand. "Dance with me."

Her eyes glittered, bottom lip disappearing between her teeth. Then she slipped her small hand into his and allowed him to lead her to the dance floor. The second she was in his arms, he let every other heavy emotion inside him, everything that had been plaguing him, slip away.

God, this woman was everything. How she'd become his everything so quickly, he wasn't sure. But he didn't need to know the how or the why, just that they'd found each other and that was it.

He lowered his mouth and pressed a kiss to her head. "This is the first year in a long, long time that I'm not dreading tomorrow."

Her head rose, expression softening. "Really?"

"Yeah. And it's because of you. Thank you."

She reached up and cupped his cheek. "I'm so glad, Nixon. You deserve to be happy."

For the first time in his adult life, he was actually starting to believe it. That maybe he wasn't the damaged soul he'd thought he was. Maybe he could have a life of his choosing that made him happy.

This time when he lowered his head, he took her mouth in a

slow, gentle kiss. His lips grazed over hers as his arms tightened around her waist.

Fuck, she annihilated him. He wanted to deepen the kiss. Hell, he wanted to drag her somewhere private, push her against the wall, and take her. It was only through a hell of a lot of self-restraint that he could even lift his mouth.

She leaned her head against his chest, right over his heart, and then he just held her. Let the music and her touch take him away from everything but her.

He wasn't sure how long they remained like that. Song after song played, and they barely moved. When it was finally time to go, it was too damn soon.

"I should get you home," he whispered.

Home…he'd called their resort "home." Because on this trip, that was exactly what it felt like. The home they'd built together.

She sighed. "Yeah. I'll just stop in the bathroom first."

He nodded, reluctantly releasing her and heading back to the table. He didn't take his gaze from her, though. The bathroom was in his direct line of sight, and he didn't look away until she stepped inside. Then he scanned the small restaurant, watching for anything that was out of place.

He'd just paid for the meal when Finley stepped out of the bathroom again. She was looking down at her phone as she crossed the space between them. Then she stopped halfway.

Suddenly, the blood drained from her face.

His skin went cold. Something was wrong.

He was across the room and in front of her in a second. He leaned to look at her phone, seeing a comment at the bottom of her most recent Instagram post.

Two warnings, and still you don't listen. You were mine, and yet you let him touch you. Now I have no choice but to take drastic action. This is no one's fault but your own. KJ.

A black rage slipped through Nixon's body, heating his blood.

That fucker. If Nixon hadn't wanted to murder the asshole before, he did now.

Finley's fingers shook as she took a screenshot of the comment, then clicked into the blank profile and blocked the person. She switched into her TikTok account, found the same comment, word for word, and did the same thing.

Even after all the comments were deleted and the asshole was blocked, her chest was heaving too quickly. Her face was so pale that it was just about white.

He cupped her cheeks. "Finley. Look at me."

She did, and all he saw was fear. It fucking shredded him.

"This asshole is not getting close to you. Do you understand?"

"He just won't leave me alone," she whispered.

"He will. Because we *will* find him, and he will regret ever harassing you. That's a promise I'm making to you." The second they touched down in the US, he was putting everything he had into finding this prick.

Her gaze held his for one full heartbeat, then finally she nodded. He kept one arm around her waist as they walked out to the car, and the other near his concealed weapon.

She was quiet the entire drive back to the resort, but he kept his fingers wrapped around her thigh, thumb grazing her. He watched the rearview mirror, making sure no one followed them. By the time they were back, some color had returned to her face. He was about to climb out when her phone rang.

She frowned. "It's Rad." She answered, putting the call on speaker. "Hey, Rad. Everything okay?"

"Actually, no. Beth's missing."

Finley's gasp was loud, and Nixon fisted his hands.

"She didn't show up for work today. I thought maybe she'd come in later, but she didn't and I couldn't get through to her. I've just gone to her place. Her car's in the drive, but she's not here. I've called the police but thought I'd check in with you as well."

Finley took a moment to answer. "No. I'm sorry, Rad. I haven't seen or talked to her today."

He blew out an audible breath. "Okay. Let me know if she makes contact."

When the call ended, she gave Nixon a desperate look. "Do you think—"

"We're not gonna play a guessing game, Finley. The police know she's missing and when they find her, we'll find out what happened to her."

The guilt on her face was so heavy, it sliced at his flesh. "Maybe he took her as some kind of punishment for me...or a replacement."

He was shaking his head before she'd finished speaking. "Don't do that to yourself. Tomorrow, we'll check in with Rad. Until then, they're gonna search for her."

She swallowed, and even though she nodded, he could see she didn't believe it. He wanted to take away her pain and guilt, but there was nothing either of them could do. Because the truth was, he felt it too. That this was probably connected.

CHAPTER 20

"*Beth?" Finley shouted the woman's name.*

People passed her in droves. Snow fell around her. But all she could see was the back of the woman in front of her.

It was Beth. She knew from the red hair. The height. The shape of her body. But she wasn't turning or acknowledging Finley's calls. It was like she couldn't hear her. Maybe with the crowd, it was too noisy, and she needed to get closer.

Finley weaved through the throngs of people, trying to close the distance between them, desperate to reach her. But every time she thought she was getting close, she'd blink and the distance would be bigger. The path more congested.

Desperation wove into her bones, causing her to shove people aside. Become frustrated at every fairgoer who blocked her path. When someone pushed her and she fell to her knees, she lost Beth completely.

Quickly, she rose and searched, her gaze finally finding her.

"Beth! Please, stop!"

But Beth didn't stop or turn, and neither did anyone else. It was like her voice didn't reach a single person. Was she even making any noise? She felt helpless.

The desperation twined into something else. Something that suffocated her. Clawed at her.

She pushed harder. Moved her feet faster. But every step felt futile. Like the distance was impossible to make up.

When Beth slipped into her trailer, relief blasted Finley's system. Because now she had a chance to reach her.

Her feet ached and the cold slapped across her flesh. She didn't stop to question why she was here at the fair. Didn't wonder where Nixon was. All she could think about was reaching Beth. Checking on her. Making sure she was okay.

It took too long, but finally, she reached the trailer. When she wrapped her fingers around the doorknob, the cold of the metal bit into her skin. She ignored it and tugged it open.

"White Christmas" played inside the trailer, its melody loud. But that wasn't what she focused on. It was Beth.

The woman stood on the other side of the space, her back facing Finley.

The air rushed out of her chest. "Beth...I'm so glad you're okay."

A second of silence passed, and nothing. No response. No movement.

Finley took a small step forward. "Beth?"

The same thing. The woman was just standing there, unnaturally still, arms hanging by her sides.

Ice slipped over Finley's skin, penetrating deep inside her right down to her bones, but it had nothing to do with the snow outside. "Beth, are you—"

The woman turned—and the air caught in Finley's throat, nausea immediately churning in her gut.

Blood...it soaked Beth's white shirt. Someone had stabbed her. Or shot her. Finley wasn't sure which. All she knew was that the woman had an open wound on her stomach. And her eyes, they were so blank, like there was no life in her.

"Wh...what happened?"

Beth stepped forward. "You did this."

Finley shook her head, her feet stumbling back a step. "No. I—"

"You came here, knowing you had a stalker. You led him straight to me."

Nausea crawled up her throat, choking her. "I didn't mean—"

"But you still did."

Finley shook her head and closed her eyes. "No. This isn't real. You're not real."

"I am."

"No." She continued to shake her head, refusing to glance up. Refusing to look at the woman in front of her.

"Look at what you've done. Finley—look at me!"

"No!" She screamed louder, the raw pain grinding at her throat. "You're not real! You're not Beth. Stay away from me!"

"Finley!"

When hands grabbed her arms, she pushed and shoved, twisting her body, begging to be released.

She needed to get away. To find Nixon. She needed him to confirm this wasn't real. Tell her everything would be okay.

The world was darkening around her when the voice twisted into something different. Something deeper. Calmer.

"Finley, you're safe. Please stop, you're gonna hurt yourself, honey."

Safe…there was that word again. And it came from Nixon.

Her eyes opened to find there was no trailer. No Beth with vacant eyes in front of her. Finley wasn't at the fair at all. She was in bed with Nixon. His fingers were wrapped around her arms, and there was so much concern on his face.

"Beth's not okay. And it's my fault!" Tears she couldn't stop built in her eyes. "It's my fault Beth's gone. He took her—I can feel it!"

Suddenly, she was tugged up and into Nixon's lap, her legs on either side of him. The second his arms came around her, she let every pent-up emotion release from her like a wave. The frustration. The anger. The fear and the guilt. All of it just came out as the tears rolled down her cheeks. She cried so long and so hard that her chest ached. Until she had nothing left.

Nixon remained silent the entire time, just holding her. Giving her everything with his gentle touch.

When the tears finally stopped falling, and any sounds that had been tearing from her chest silenced, he pulled back, his hands on her upper arms. "Even if she is in trouble, this isn't your fault. Nothing that has happened involving this asshole is your fault. It's all on *him*. Do you understand me?"

He'd said that before, but God, it was hard to believe. It felt like it was all on her. "If I hadn't come here—"

"If he *did* take her? Then if you hadn't come, he would have just found another way to torment you. Another person to hurt trying to reach you. Because that's what sick assholes do. They use whatever means they can to destroy you."

"I want this to be over. I want Beth to be safe and for him to be gone."

And not just arrested or behind bars. She wanted him gone permanently so he couldn't hurt her or anyone else again.

"Me too, honey. And he will be. I swear."

She was shaking her head before he'd finished. "You can't promise that—"

"I can and I am. I promise on my life that we will take him down and he will never mess with you again."

There was so much certainty in his voice…and she needed it. She needed *him*.

She slid her hands up his chest, desperate for more of his calm. His goodness. His safety.

Leaning forward, she pressed a small kiss to his bare chest. Then another, this time right over his heart.

"Finley…" Her name was a whisper on his lips, but it almost sounded torn.

She kissed his chest again, his heart thumping under her lips. Slowly, she trailed up his powerful body. Up his neck, his cheek. He remained still the entire time. Even his breath stilled.

When she reached his mouth, she nipped at his lip. Ran her

tongue along the seam of his mouth. Then she whispered, "Pull me back from the edge."

His eyes darkened. Then his mouth took over, and he pulled her back to him.

* * *

NIXON LOST HIMSELF IN HER. Her lips. Her taste.

When she tightened her legs, grinding her core against him, the blood roared between his ears. She was soft and warm and his. So his.

Her lips parted, and he slipped his tongue inside her mouth.

God, this woman destroyed him. Tugged him apart bit by bit, twisting him into something different, something better.

He reached for the bottom of her top and tugged it over her head. Then he cupped her bare breast. When that wasn't enough, he dipped his head and pulled her pretty pink nipple into his mouth, sucking.

Finley gasped, her fingers sliding into his hair, pulling, as her hips ground against him.

He ran his tongue over the bud, playing with her before switching to the other breast.

When she pressed a hand to his cheek, pulling him back to her, he released her nipple and returned to her mouth, their tongues melding once again.

Fuck, he ached for her.

Without removing her mouth from his, she pushed up and slipped her panties down her hips and thighs before returning to him.

Immediately, his hand went to her core, and he stroked her clit. She whimpered and he did it again. Every sound this woman made gutted him.

He switched his thumb to her clit and moved a finger to her

entrance. Her body stilled. He nipped at her bottom lip as he pushed inside.

Her moan was loud, intoxicating. He did it again, thrusting his finger in and out of her, watching the emotions slip over her expressive face.

"Nixon," she breathed.

His name on her lips was a gift.

She reached down between them and slipped her hand inside his briefs. Then her fingers wrapped around his cock. His muscles tensed, his action stilling. For a moment, he couldn't move. Couldn't breathe. Then her hand moved from base to tip. Exploring. Playing.

A deep guttural groan escaped his throat. "Finley…you need to stop."

He slipped his finger out of her and gripped her hips firmly with both hands.

Her mouth went to his ear. "With you, I can never stop."

She leaned over and grabbed a foil from the drawer. She tore it open with her lips before tugging him out. The air hissed from his lips as she slid it over his cock.

Then she lifted her hips and positioned his tip at her entrance. His world narrowed to just her. Slowly, so slowly it nearly killed him, she slid down, her walls stretching around him.

Fuck, she was so wet for him.

When he was seated deep inside her, she didn't move. Instead, she cupped both his cheeks, her breasts pressed to his chest, eyes bleeding into him as she whispered, "You have my heart, Nixon Reid."

The words seared him. "You own me, Finley."

Her eyes heated, then her head dropped, and she kissed him. Her mouth was still sealed to his when her hips rose, thrusting back down fast.

He growled. She did it again.

At every thrust, her breasts dragged against his chest and her walls hugged his cock. He wrapped an arm around her waist, and with his other hand, cupped the back of her head, unable to stop kissing her. Tasting her. He helped her lift and lower, bringing her down harder every time she returned to him.

It was everything. *She* was everything. The miracle gift for a holiday he'd always dreaded. The one sent to save him. He was almost scared to let her go in case this wasn't real. In case she hadn't really entered his life and changed everything.

He sucked and nibbled her bottom lip, then kissed down her jaw. She threw her head back, and he took advantage, latching onto her neck. He slipped his hand to her breast, cupping her. Finding her nipple and pinching.

A shudder ran down her back. He did it again.

When that wasn't enough, he continued to trail that hand down her body, finding her clit and rolling it with his thumb.

Her cry was a strangled scream.

She thrust harder. Faster. He continued to circle her clit until finally, she broke. Shattered around him violently, her walls throbbing against his cock.

He continued to lift his hips as she kept thrusting, until he broke with her. Came apart hard, violently.

Still, he didn't release her. He held her close, unable to let her go.

Holding this woman was like a drug—sweet and addictive.

Even as they stilled, her shudders continued to roll through her body, into him.

He was still inside her when her lips moved to his ear. "Nixon…it's three a.m." Then she pressed a small kiss to his shoulder. "Merry Christmas."

For the first time in years, those words didn't crush him. Didn't pull him so deep into darkness that he couldn't see the light.

His arms around her tightened. "Merry Christmas, honey."

CHAPTER 21

$\mathcal{F}$inley leaned her head back against the passenger seat.

Home. Today, they were going home. It felt crazy that it was less than a week and a half ago that she'd arrived in Fallen Ridge. So little time had passed, yet she felt like a completely different person from the one who'd arrived.

Nixon reached over from behind the wheel and slipped his fingers through hers. Then, like it was the most natural thing in the world, he lifted her hand and kissed the back of it.

Her heart thumped. Man, he was perfect. Perfect for her. Almost as if he was the missing piece of her life.

"You okay?" he asked quietly.

"Yeah. Just thinking about everything that's happened in the last week. It's been…a lot."

"Not all of it was terrible, I hope."

The corners of her mouth twitched. "No. Not all of it."

The moments spent with this man were far from terrible. Sure, he'd ground her gears a few times, and the relationship between them hadn't come easy. But nothing worth keeping usually did.

She turned her head to watch the trees pass outside the window. The snow hit the ground like tiny clouds falling from the sky.

"Do you know this was my first time in Canada?" she asked quietly.

"Really? And what do you think?"

"It's beautiful. I want to come back and make more memories." Drown out the bad ones, because even though there was so much to love about this trip, her stalker was like the gray cloud that hovered over her head. "I hate that we're leaving before we know where Beth is."

Her nightmare from last night came back to her, chilling her skin, making dread well up in her stomach. Had the dream been right? Had the asshole who was stalking her taken Beth because of Finley?

Nixon's fingers tightened around her hand. "The police force here will find her, and we'll keep in contact with Rad so we can learn any updates."

She nodded, even though that heavy feeling inside her was still there, sitting on her chest, weighing her down. Every minute that passed where they didn't locate her, Beth's chances of being found alive decreased.

"How are you feeling about the flight?" Nixon asked, pulling her out of her thoughts.

She shrugged. "Compared to everything else that's happened on this trip, that feels like the easy part."

"So your phobia's cured?"

She laughed. "Definitely not. I'm sure the second we take off, I'll be grabbing your arm so hard I cut off the circulation."

He chuckled. "Grab me as tightly as you need to, honey."

Man, she loved it when he used that endearment.

She was gazing out the window again when her phone rang from the middle console. She frowned and lifted it, seeing Rad's name flash across the screen.

Her pulse picked up, hope dancing in her chest. "Rad, any news on Beth?"

"No, unfortunately not." The hope fizzled. "I'm actually calling because the police are here. They want to ask you a couple of questions before you get on the plane."

Right on cue, a police radio sounded in the background.

Her gaze shifted to the time. They still had a few hours before their flight. They'd left the hotel early because Nixon had wanted to get going. But it was Christmas Day. Would it be busy at the fair? "I don't know if I feel comfortable walking through a busy fair today."

"Being Christmas Day, the fair's closed today."

She hadn't known they were closing today. Not that it was a surprise, since most people would be home with their families.

"Even if it wasn't Christmas Day, it wouldn't have felt right remaining open while Beth's missing."

"I can understand that." She ran her thumb over Nixon's hand. "Okay. Sure. We can stop at the fair." Nixon frowned at her. "We'll only have time for a quick stop, though. So we can catch our flight."

"Not a problem. I don't think this will take long. We're in the warehouse on the second floor. The heating's better in here."

"Okay. See you soon." She hung up and turned to Nixon. "The police want to ask us some questions before we get on the plane. The fair's closed, so we don't need to worry about other people being around."

The muscles in his arms tensed, but he nodded, turning the rental car around and heading toward the fair.

She was sure he didn't like it because he just wanted to get her out of here. She'd felt it in him. Hell, he'd all but woken up and flown into action this morning. Packing their bags and getting out of the resort.

She wished she could make today better for him. It was Christmas, and she wanted to give him only good holiday memories. But all either of them could think about was this stalker and getting away from him.

As they drove, she stroked his arm. "Are you nervous about when we get back to the States?" The words fell from her mouth before she could pull them back. But then, it wasn't a surprise. It was basically all she'd been thinking about lately.

"No. Are you?"

She almost laughed. "Yes. We haven't worked out whether I'm coming to you or you're coming to me or if we're doing a long-distance relationship…"

"You're coming to me."

She swung her gaze to him, eyes widening. He said it with such certainty, like it had already been decided.

He lifted a shoulder. "I mean, when we said we were gonna do this, I just assumed that's how it would work. We haven't caught the stalker. He has your address. And you can work from anywhere. Plus, my place has a lot of security."

Some of the excitement fizzled from her chest. He wanted her to live with him for security reasons. She shouldn't be sad…he wanted them to be together. But a part of her couldn't help but wish he'd said something more intimate.

"Do you *want* to move in with me?" he asked.

"Yes." Of course she did. But not because of security. And she didn't want that to be his reason either. She plastered a smile on her face. "You'll have to help me pack, though."

He squeezed her hand. "I happen to be an excellent packer."

When they pulled up at the fair, Nixon parked beside a police car. There were also two other cars in the parking lot, a blue Toyota and a black Ford.

They both climbed out. When she looked out at the empty fairgrounds, her nightmare came back to her. Her gaze shifted to the trailer, and an involuntary shudder ran down her spine.

Nixon stood beside her, slipping an arm around her waist. "Are you okay?"

She nodded quickly. Maybe too quickly. "Yeah. It's just a bit… eerie when there's no one here. It feels wrong."

"Come on. Let's get this over with so we can go home."

They walked to the large warehouse. When they stepped inside, she immediately wanted to sink into the warmth.

The space was dark and musty, with sheets over what she assumed was a front desk, right before a small corridor. It looked like no one had come in here in years.

Nixon's arm tightened around her as he led her to the wide staircase. When they reached the top, Finley frowned. It looked to be one big open room. Work desks were scattered around the space, each bare except for the dust that had collected on top.

But where was Rad? Where were the police? And why was it so quiet?

She started to step forward, but Nixon grabbed her arm, tugging her back. She opened her mouth to ask him what was wrong but stopped at the sudden squawk of a police radio.

"Darren…Joy…are you there?"

Where had that come from?

Her heart started to thump, dread pooling in her belly, when she noticed movement at the back of the cavernous room.

Before she could comprehend what was happening, Nixon shoved her to the floor behind a desk, covering her body with his own as a bullet slammed into the wall behind them.

For a moment, shock rendered her still. Then she lifted her head—and something caught her attention.

The blood drained from her face.

There, only a few feet away, lay two police officers, both on their stomachs…blood seeping from wounds in their backs.

* * *

THE ASSHOLE WAS SHOOTING at them.

Fuck.

These desks wouldn't do shit to protect them. A bullet would go straight fucking through the wood. He had to get Finley out of here, *now*.

He pulled his gun from the holster, then shifted his body to the side, making sure he positioned himself between her and the shooter. "You need to run, Finley!"

It was like she didn't hear him. Her attention was focused on something across the room. He followed her gaze, cursing at the sight of the dead uniformed officers.

He grabbed her shoulder firmly. "Finley! Look at me." When she finally did, her eyes were unfocused. "I'm giving you the keys. I want you to run to the car, lock yourself inside, and get away."

She was shaking her head before he finished speaking. "No. I'm not leaving you."

"You *are*. Because I'm gonna end this asshole."

"Nixon—"

He pushed the car keys into her hand. "Go!"

She gave him one last look before rising to her hands and knees and crawling back to the stairs. The second she started moving, he rose slightly and started firing at the back corner of the room.

Nixon rushed to the next desk. He kept firing as he moved, creeping from desk to desk to close the space between them.

He wasn't letting this guy go. He'd follow her back to the States. Torment her further. And she'd forever be looking over her shoulder.

Hell no. That wasn't happening. This was ending today.

When the return fire came, Nixon took cover, dropping flat to his stomach behind a desk.

He took a moment to breathe. To let the rage flow through his blood like fast-moving acid.

He shuffled to the other side of the table, then rose and fired, aiming at the hand. A loud curse sounded, but the gun didn't drop.

He'd only nicked him.

Nixon rushed to the next desk. He was so fucking close now. He waited for that arm to pop out again, and the second it did, he fired—this time getting a clean shot of the forearm.

The guy howled, the gun dropping to the floor. Nixon raced forward and lunged, grabbing him around the middle and sending him crashing to the floor.

He wore a balaclava over his head, and Nixon shoved a gun to his temple.

Immediately, the guy lifted his hands. "Don't shoot! Please!"

Nixon's brows tugged together. That voice…it was familiar. And his eyes…

He grabbed the balaclava and pulled it over his head.

The fury inside Nixon grew, threatening to erupt.

"Rad?" Nixon growled. "It was you? All this fucking time, it was you!"

Rad shook his head vigorously. "No! No, please! I was here with police! We were waiting for you and this guy came up here and shot the cops!"

"What are you talking about?"

"He killed them and told me he had Beth. That if I didn't kill you when you got here, he'd kill her *and* me!"

"Why the fuck would I believe that? You could have waited for us to get here and asked for our help. You could have called police. Hell, there are a million things you could have done other than shooting at me."

The man started to shake, tears running down his face in a fast stream. "It's true. I swear, it's true. I just did what he said because I didn't want to die."

Ice started to filter into Nixon's limbs…at the way this man was breaking down below him. It wasn't fake. Rad was a decoy… the stalker had known that Nixon would stay to end him. That he'd send Finley away to safety…

Suddenly, a gunshot fired outside.

A fear like Nixon had never known coursed through his body. He grabbed Rad's gun and took off.

CHAPTER 22

Finley's heart beat hard in her chest, her feet pounding the stairs as she ran down. Every step she took away from Nixon felt wrong. Like she was deserting him. But if she stayed, she'd be a distraction. He would have one eye on her instead of two on the enemy. He needed to concentrate, and to do that, she needed to get away.

When she reached the bottom of the stairs, she beelined for the door, all but falling out of it. The cold shot through her system, but for once she barely noticed it.

Run to the car, lock yourself inside, and get away.

Nixon's words repeated in her head. It was all that kept her moving. She couldn't let them stop. Because then she'd turn around and return to him.

She sprinted toward the bridge, a sob clawing at her throat, begging to break free. Even from here, she could hear the sound of the bullets—like small explosions. And every one of them made her flinch. Made fear catapult her belly into panic.

She shook her head, whispering words that she needed to hear. That he'd be okay. That once she was in the car, she'd call the police and get him help.

At the thought of the police, her mind flicked to the two dead officers in the warehouse.

Dead. The guy had killed them.

She choked back another sob.

She'd just reached the bridge when something by the rental car caught her attention. Movement that flickered from behind the vehicle.

Her feet slammed to a halt as something tight and uncomfortable coiled inside her.

Could there be two of them working together?

She took a small step back. Then another. Everything inside her screamed at her to run. Get away.

Another flash of movement.

She didn't think—she just turned and ran. Moved her body faster than she'd thought possible, the air soaring in and out of her lungs as her arms pumped. She had no idea where she was going. She couldn't lead him back to Nixon, not when he already had another threat to focus on.

She'd just passed the warehouse when a bullet struck the ground near her feet. She screamed, her feet stumbling, body flying to the ground. She was only down for a second before she sprang back up and forced herself to move faster.

At the snowman-building site, she looked around in a panic. She was close to the woods. Would she make it?

She lifted a heavy shovel from one of the barrels, then cut diagonally across the area toward the fence. She was almost there when something inside screamed at her to stop. Hide. Take cover.

The fear was overwhelming. Choking her. Drowning her.

She stepped behind a tall snowman and tried to muffle her loud breathing.

That's when she heard it. The small crack of a branch breaking underfoot, near the entrance to the site. Her pulse picked up, a small shake starting in her fingers that had nothing to do with the cold.

"I've waited a long time for this, Finley."

Nausea rolled through her at the sound of the deep, unfamiliar voice. At the way it sank into her chest, spreading like wildfire.

"When you posted that you were coming to this Christmas fair, I knew it was the perfect place for us to finally meet and start our forever. You wrote about how much you loved Christmas. I've always loved Christmas too."

She tightened her fingers around the shovel, hating that his voice moved closer, erasing the space between them.

"You kept deleting my comments on your posts and blocking me. I thought maybe you just didn't understand my intentions. How much I care for you. So I left you the mistletoe. And *still* you continued to push me away, refusing to interact with me."

God, the guy was a psychopath.

"Then you let *him* touch you!"

She swallowed the bile in her throat, begging the fear inside her to remain silent.

"And I started thinking…maybe you didn't *deserve* the life I had planned for us after all. Maybe, if I couldn't have you, no one could."

When a bullet fired, her breath stopped, and she had to cover her mouth to stop the gasp. Then there was another.

It took three bullets for her to realize the guy was shooting the snowmen…trying to find her.

Jesus Christ.

Fear spiraled up her spine, causing acid to build in her throat.

She crept as far to one side of the snowman as possible, not sure if that would save her from a bullet, but it was all she could do.

She tightened her fingers around the shovel yet again as her gaze moved around the area. Should she make a run for it? If she stayed where she was, she was a sitting duck.

Her gaze shifted to the fence again. It wasn't far, but if the guy wanted to shoot her, there was no way she'd make it.

When a bullet fired through the snowman she was hiding behind, she barely stifled the cry.

If she hadn't moved those few inches, she'd have been shot. Maybe killed.

Suddenly, his footsteps were so close she could hear his breathing.

Before she could overthink it, she swung the shovel as hard as she could and hit the guy in the head.

He cried out and fell to the ground, but the gun remained in his hand. She tried to run, but he lunged, grabbing her ankle, causing her to topple. She grunted and kicked at his hand, then his face.

When her gaze collided with his, something niggled at her memory. She'd seen him before. Where, exactly, she wasn't sure.

She didn't stop to think about it, though. She kicked again, her foot colliding with his nose.

He cursed loudly, grabbing his face as blood streamed from his nose. She jumped up and ran, throwing herself over the perimeter fence and slipping into the woods. She tried to follow the paths where the snow had melted so she wouldn't leave prints. The shovel remained firmly in her fingers. It was so heavy, probably slowing her down, but it was the only weapon she had.

She ran so far and so fast that her lungs burned and her legs ached. But she didn't stop.

She was just weaving through the trees when she saw something black behind a tree. Her feet slowed. A boot. Step by step, she moved closer...until she saw all of Beth's body.

* * *

Nixon's blood ran cold when he stepped outside. Where the fuck was Finley?

He moved toward the parking lot, weapon raised. Other than his rental car and the police car, there were two other vehicles in the lot. One of them had to be Rad's, and the other…?

His gaze went to the Ford with the tinted windows. They were so dark that he couldn't see inside.

Was that the fucker's car?

Rage pumped through his veins. Rage at the asshole for setting this up. For targeting her. And rage at himself for letting the woman out of his goddamn sight.

He kept low as he neared the vehicle, then shot at the driver's-side window. Nothing. He moved closer, reaching through the broken glass and opening the door.

When he saw the empty interior, not just the front but the back, his gut clenched.

A shot sounded in the distance.

His world stopped.

Nixon ran, crossing the bridge and pounding through the snow.

As he moved, he pulled his phone from his pocket and called the police. He didn't stay on the line for long, just made sure they knew there was a shooter at the fairgrounds and two officers were down before hanging up.

More gunshots. Each one felt like a hit to his own chest.

But when the shots stopped, he suddenly wanted them back, because the silence was so much worse. The silence made every one of his fears come to life and consume him.

When he reached the snowman-building section of the fair, his heart jumped into his throat. Bullets had clearly been fired through the snowmen—but why? The only thing that stopped him from losing his damn mind over the possibilities was the fact that she wasn't here, which meant maybe no bullets had hit Finley.

His gaze zeroed in on blood in the white snow. He ran toward it, seeing the imprint of a body. Not Finley's. It was too big.

Did that mean the blood wasn't hers?

He lifted his gaze, spotting a few more specks of blood toward the fence. She'd gotten away…and he'd given chase.

Nixon sprinted toward the tree line, then into the woods, ignoring the way branches slapped his skin and his feet sank into the earth.

Finley was all he could think about.

He scanned the trees, desperately searching for her. The farther he moved into the woods, the more he silenced his steps and the harder he listened.

He wanted noise, dammit! Something to guide him in the right direction—toward Finley.

But there was nothing. No whispers of movement. No rustle of leaves.

Frustration was about to overwhelm him when he saw it—a flash of color. Red.

Finley had been wearing red.

Not caring about quieting his movements any longer, Nixon ran toward it, pumping his limbs hard and fast. When he neared a huge tree, a shovel suddenly swung toward him.

He dodged the makeshift weapon easily, grabbing the handle.

Finley's eyes collided with his, the air rushing from her lungs. "Nixon!" She dropped the shovel and fell into his arms, the sound she made something between a whimper and a cry.

He took a moment to breathe her in. To allow the full weight of his relief to sit inside him. Calm some of the storm.

Then his gaze shot down to see a body—Beth. She was still and pale, dried blood on her hairline where someone had obviously hit her.

The fucking animal.

When he pulled back, he studied Finley's face. "What happened? Where is he?"

"I don't know! I hit him with the shovel, then ran into the woods. I stopped when I saw Beth. She's alive but her heartbeat's faint. I dragged her behind this tree and have been hiding here ever since. I can't leave her!"

Fuck. Her stalker was out here somewhere. But where?

The second the question entered his head, a branch crunched somewhere behind him. He pushed Finley to the ground behind the tree, then crouched beside her and lowered his voice to a whisper. "Whatever happens, stay down. Okay?"

Her eyes were wide and skin pale, but she nodded.

Another crunch, this one louder. Closer.

"Did you find Beth, Finley?" a male voice shouted.

Nixon's teeth ground together.

"I took her because I knew how much pain it would cause you. I also knew she'd come in handy…which she did. That idiot cousin of hers did everything I asked."

Nixon's fingers tightened around his Glock. He wanted to kill this asshole.

The guy was still moving closer, and while Nixon wanted him as far from Finley as possible, another part of him welcomed the closing of the distance. Because Nixon wanted to tear the guy apart with his bare hands.

"Did that asshole friend of yours find you? Or is he dead?" the guy shouted. "I kind of hope he found you, because that means I get to gut him right in front of your eyes. Show you just how much more of a man I am…everything you missed out on because you whored yourself out to him!"

Nixon's vision blackened, the anger inside him threatening to overflow into violence.

"We could have been great together. Now—you die."

When a bullet hit the ground beside the tree, Nixon cursed.

The asshole knew where they were.

When a second bullet hit, Nixon eased his gun around the tree. The guy saw him a split second before he fired and dropped to the ground, immediately raising his pistol to return fire, but Nixon was already behind the tree.

Then steps. Quick ones. Before the man even came into view, Nixon kicked out a leg, sending him to the ground. He swung his weapon around, but the asshole kicked it out of his hands.

Nixon cursed and dove forward, grabbing the asshole's wrist before he could aim the pistol, slamming his hand to the ground. He snapped his head forward, smashing his forehead into the man's already broken nose.

The guy howled, fresh blood pouring down his face. Nixon immediately threw an elbow toward his cheek, but he rolled, smashing Nixon to his back.

"I'm gonna kill you for taking her from me!" he growled, yanking a knife from a sheath at his ankle.

Nixon was reaching for his wrist even as the shovel suddenly came down on the guy's head, causing him to grunt and drop to the ground.

Still, the fucker didn't stay down. He cursed and rolled toward his fallen gun. Nixon wrenched the pistol he'd taken from Rad from his holster.

The guy was lifting his own pistol when Nixon fired, putting a bullet between his eyes.

He dropped...then there was silence.

Nixon rose to his feet and stepped toward Finley on heavy legs. Carefully, he slipped the shovel from her fingers and dropped it to the dirt.

He gently cupped her face. "Hey." It took a beat, but she finally lifted her gaze to his. "Are you okay?"

She nodded, voice shaking. "Yeah. Are you?"

He was far from fucking okay. She'd come too close to getting hurt. He gave her crumbs of the truth. "No. But holding you is making me feel better."

She nodded, the air rushing in and out of her chest. "He's dead," she whispered.

Nixon tugged her into his arms. "He's dead."

CHAPTER 23

Finley watched from the parking lot as paramedics carried Beth on a stretcher from the woods. Her feet twitched to go to her. Check in. She hated that the woman had been hurt because of her. Hated that she was still unconscious, and they had no idea if the hit to her head was her only injury.

The only thing she was holding on to, her one reprieve, was that the woman still had a heartbeat.

Finley leaned against Nixon's side, needing to borrow just a bit of his strength. "Do you think she'll be okay?"

His arm tightened around her waist. "I don't know, honey. But I hope so. I overheard paramedics talking in the woods. Words like dehydration, blood loss, and concussion were mentioned. Also, her body temperature is low."

She swallowed, hating everything Nixon had just said.

"But they didn't think she'd slept in the woods all night, because she probably wouldn't be alive right now if she had. And also because police searched that exact spot yesterday."

"Why would he have left her there then?" she asked, unable to keep the question to herself.

"Maybe he wanted her close in case Rad didn't believe him? Needed to show the guy evidence that he had her."

Her belly rolled at the mention of Rad. She still couldn't believe what he'd done. Yes, he'd shot at them as a means to protect himself and his cousin, but he should have chosen another option.

As Beth was loaded into the ambulance, two more stretchers rolled into the parking lot, but this time from the old warehouse building. These stretchers had sheets pulled over the bodies.

A shudder raced down her spine. A part of her was still in disbelief that the guy had gone so far as to kill two police officers. From comments on her social media to murder…it was crazy.

"None of this feels real," she whispered, speaking her thoughts out loud.

A kiss pressed to her head. "I know, honey. At least he's dead."

He *was* dead. But that didn't take away from the damage he'd done.

When police came out of the warehouse with Rad in cuffs, she straightened. He almost looked unrecognizable from the man she'd met a week ago. His chin was on his chest, and he looked… dejected. In shock.

Was he comprehending the error of his ways now?

Rad was almost at the police car when he stopped, head lifting, gaze colliding with hers. He tried to move toward her, but the officers stopped him.

"I'm sorry," he said, loud enough for his voice to cross the distance. "He said he'd kill Beth if I didn't do what he wanted. I wasn't planning to kill either of you. Just shoot in your direction. I thought that would appease him enough to leave me alone…to let Beth go."

She frowned as Rad was pushed into the back of a police car.

The second he was out of sight, the air rushed from her chest. "I know this sounds crazy, but I almost feel sorry for him."

Nixon tensed. "Why?"

She shrugged one shoulder. "Because two police officers were shot and killed in front of him, and he was threatened. I feel guilty that he got caught up in this because of me."

Nixon turned, cupping her cheeks. "Not because of you. Because of that asshole who targeted you. And the second Rad had the opportunity, he should have called the police. Hell, he should have shot your stalker the second the weapon was put in his hand."

She nodded, knowing he was right but still hating it.

When a police officer stepped in front of them, Finley glanced up.

"Hi. I'm Officer Phillip, and I'd like to hear both your accounts of what happened today."

* * *

NIXON LISTENED with gritted teeth as Finley gave her version of events. He already knew most of it, but hearing it hit different. And listening to her describe how the asshole had chased her… shot at the fucking snowmen, trying to find her…it gutted him.

The only part of the story he liked was the ending, where the asshole got a bullet in the fucking head. He also didn't mind the parts where she'd nailed the fucker with the shovel and broken his nose.

Damn, he was proud of her. Her strength. Her smarts. The way she'd dragged Beth to a new location, then protected a woman she barely knew.

It just cemented everything Nixon already knew about Finley…that she was fucking made for him.

The officer nodded as she finished up, the pen in his hand moving across the paper.

When the final stretcher was carried out of the woods, the asshole's body clearly underneath, the officer looked up, then excused himself to meet the officers walking with the body.

Finley was so damn tense beside him. All he wanted to do was give her just a shred of peace. He lowered his mouth to the top of her head and kissed her. "He can't hurt you anymore."

"I know. I just…I want to know who he is. I want to know why he did what he did."

Nixon wanted to know all of that as well. He knew the guy was a sick fuck, but he still wanted to know everything there was to know about the man. What had motivated him to target Finley? Had he done this to anyone else?

Nixon watched as one of the cops handed a card to Officer Phillip. He looked down at it before walking away. He was passing them when Nixon called him over.

"Do you know who he was?" Nixon asked, needing more information.

The policeman held out the man's driver's license. "Kevin Jones. We ran him through the system. He's a thirty-three-year-old truck driver from Tacoma, Washington. He's in the system for stalking and harassing before. He was diagnosed with borderline personality disorder and has a health care regimen in place. We suspect he went off his medication."

Finley blinked, staring hard at the driver's license.

When she gasped, he looked down at her. "What is it, honey?"

"I remember where I've seen him before."

Nixon's brows flickered. She'd seen him somewhere? "Where?"

"On the plane as I was walking to my seat. He was coming from the other direction and bumped into my shoulder."

The asshole had been on the same damn plane as them? "Did you announce to your followers when you were flying out?"

She swallowed and nodded, regret darkening her eyes. "Not the exact flight, just the day I was leaving. But he knew where I lived, so he probably also knew where I was flying from and found the information for the flight to Fallen Ridge."

So the asshole had booked a last-minute seat on the same

plane as her. Suddenly, Nixon wanted to kill him a second time. For harassing Finley. Scaring her. Presuming she was his just because he wanted her.

"That would have given him enough to figure it out," the officer said with a nod. "But he won't cause you any more trouble. I'll need you both to come into the station for a more formal interview, I'm afraid."

Nixon nodded, and the guy walked away. They'd long missed their flight anyway. Not that Nixon minded. It had been a long-ass day, and the last thing she needed was to get on a plane.

When Finley was quiet for a beat too long, he shifted in front of her and cupped her cheek. "What's going on in your head?"

"I just made it so easy for him."

She was blaming herself again. And fuck, he hated that. "Social media is your work, and he abused the access you gave him to your life because he was sick. If he hadn't acted here in Fallen Ridge, he would have done it back in your hometown. Or wherever your next trip was. He would have found a way to get to you."

At her shudder, he tugged her into his arms.

She lay her head on his shoulder. "Thank you for finding me in those woods and saving me."

He shook his head. "No. Thank you for fighting the asshole off. If I'd lost you—"

"You didn't. And I didn't lose you. We're both here and alive."

And damn he was grateful for that. "God, I love you, Finley."

Her gaze rose, eyes widening. "Love?"

"Yeah, honey. I love you."

She smiled. "I love you too."

He'd been craving those words.

His head dropped and he kissed her, letting the softness of her lips and the heat of her body soothe every little part of him that was still feeling the pain and torment of almost losing her today.

CHAPTER 24

Finley's heart thudded hard and loud in her chest as she handed the flight attendant her ticket.

It would be fine. A quick flight and she'd be home.

The woman handed it back, and Finley moved down the aisle, passing business class and stepping into economy. She breathed a sigh of relief when she took her middle seat in the front row. It wasn't the aisle, but at least it wasn't the window. A little win.

Quickly, she uncapped her small bottle of pills and slipped a Xanax between her lips before swallowing it down with water.

"Nervous flyer?" a woman asked as she stepped past her and lowered into the window seat.

That was an understatement. "The worst. Although, I don't feel as terrible on this flight as usual."

"What was the magic trick?"

She could have laughed, even though there was nothing funny about the situation. It wasn't so much a magic trick, as much as it was experiencing a lifetime of fear in less than two weeks. "No trick. I just had a few things put in perspective this holiday season."

She pulled out her phone, spotting a text from Andi. Her best friend had been messaging a lot to check on Finley since her hospital stay, but also because she was worried about her older brother, Erik, and his new partner. Apparently, a lot had also happened in Redwood while she'd been gone. His new partner had been targeted by some not-so-great people. From what Andi had told her, it had been a close call on getting her to safety.

She hurried to write a response before flicking her phone to flight mode.

The woman beside her gasped quietly, then whispered. "Oh my gosh, he's huge!"

Finley looked up, and the smile that spread across her face was easy and instant. Nixon. He settled in the aisle seat beside her, pressing a kiss to her cheek before fastening his seat belt.

"Everything okay?" she asked. He'd insisted on hanging back and being one of the last to board. Some security measure of his.

"Yeah, everything's fine." He met her gaze. "How are you doing?"

She lifted a shoulder. "Well, I'm not harassing the stranger in the aisle seat to switch with me."

The corners of his mouth twitched. "It's a safety thing."

"After I found out who you were, I assumed as much. *Before* I found out who you were, I just thought you were a bit of a jerk."

"I *am* a bit of a jerk."

She laughed and shook her head. "Only when you want to be. Luckily, I love you anyway."

His eyes heated.

When the flight attendant came to stand in the aisle and began going through the safety talk, Finley started a fast tap of her foot. She focused on remaining calm. On breathing. What really helped, though, was Nixon's hand on top of hers. The way his thumb grazed her skin. The heat of his shoulder against her own.

The fear was there on takeoff, but it wasn't as bad as it usually was.

Nixon lowered his mouth to her ear and whispered, "Breathe."

So she did. Because that was just the effect the man had on her. If he told her to jump out of the plane, she'd probably do it for him.

When they were finally in the air, she pulled out her phone, sighing when she saw the social media apps. She hadn't deactivated them yet, but she would. First, she needed to make an announcement to her followers.

"You thinking about your business?"

She looked up at Nixon. "Yeah. I thought I'd feel sadder about letting go of everything I built. But I don't. The change feels right."

He gently brushed some hair behind her ear. "You still gonna teach others to do what you did?"

"Yes. And I'm looking forward to the pivot in my career. There are so many people who are looking for this information and trying to build a platform. I've already got so many ideas, not just for working one-on-one with clients but also creating courses so I can reach as many people as possible."

"I love that you're looking forward to it."

She beamed at him. "I really am. I'm also excited about moving in with you."

When they were back at the resort, she'd reluctantly mentioned that, since the threat was gone, he didn't have to move her into his home. The second the words left her mouth, his features had hardened and he'd proceeded to let her know there was no way he was letting her live anywhere *but* with him, ever.

Nixon lowered his head. "I can't wait."

He kissed her, taking her away from everything but him.

* * *

A CALM NIXON had rarely felt in his life seeped through his bones at the weight of Finley's head on his shoulder. At the sigh of her soft breaths as she slept.

Yeah, she was sleeping on another two-hour flight, and there wasn't a single part of him that wanted to wake her.

This trip had been a whirlwind. He'd found things that he'd never thought he'd find. Love. Peace. A hope for the future he'd never fucking felt before.

Since the day his sister had died, he'd distanced himself from everyone in this world with the exception of his SEAL team. It had been an intentional move to keep himself from being hurt or from hurting others. But bit by bit, this woman had weaved her way into his world, cracking the protective shell around his heart. And now there was no going back. No letting her go or falling back into his old ways.

She'd changed him. And become so damn vital, he couldn't even conceive of a life without her.

The entire time she slept, the slight pressure of her cheek soothed him, the softness of her body heating his blood.

It wasn't until they were on approach, and the pilot came over the speaker, that he cupped her cheek. "Honey. We're landing."

Her eyes opened slowly, then she looked up at him, gaze soft before humor danced in the brown depths. "Oh my gosh...I fell asleep again."

He kissed the top of her head. "You did. But I kind of liked it."

"Well, I'm sure you liked it more than the first time I did it, back when I was a stranger."

He shrugged. "I kind of liked it then, too. Not that I would have admitted that out loud."

Something crossed her face, some unreadable emotion.

He ran his thumb over her bottom lip. "What is it, honey?"

"I was just thinking about what a mess yesterday was. I hate that it happened on Christmas Day. It gives you more reason to hate the holiday."

He shook his head. "Yesterday wasn't all bad."

Her brow furrowed.

"Not only did we eliminate the asshole," he continued, "but it was the first day you said you loved me. And the first day I said it out loud to you. I haven't told anyone I love them in a very long time."

A thin sheen of tears filled her eyes. "Nixon…"

"Yesterday was the start of our forever, Finley. And I promise you…I will love you and protect you until the day I die. I am so damn grateful you came into my life."

She wet her lips, swiping at a tear that spilled down her cheek. Then she smiled. "So we're a bit of a Christmas miracle, aren't we? Like eggnog?"

He chuckled, lowering his head. "*You* are a Christmas miracle. Eggnog is *not*."

Then he kissed her. Lost himself in her. Drowned in her.

CLICK HERE to dive into the Beautiful Pieces series featuring Erik Hunter - book one ERIK'S SALVATION!

ALSO BY NYSSA KATHRYN

PROJECT ARMA SERIES

Uncovering Project Arma

Luca

Eden

Asher

Mason

Wyatt

Bodie

Oliver

Kye

BLUE HALO SERIES

Logan

Jason

Blake

Flynn

Aidan

Tyler

Callum

Liam

MERCY RING

Jackson

Declan

Cole

Ryker

BEAUTIFUL PIECES

(series ongoing)

Erik's Salvation

Erik's Redemption

Erik's Refuge

SHORT CHRISTMAS STORY

Hidden Shadows

RECKLESS SERIES

(series ongoing)

Reckless Hope

Reckless Trust

JOIN my newsletter and be the first to find out about sales and new releases! CLICK HERE

ABOUT THE AUTHOR

Nyssa Kathryn is a romantic suspense author. She lives in South Australia with her daughter and hubby and takes every chance she can to be plotting and writing. Always an avid reader of romance novels, she considers alpha males and happily-ever-afters to be her jam.

Don't forget to follow Nyssa and never miss another release.

Facebook | Instagram | Amazon | Goodreads